BONE

HANDBOOK

BY JEFF SMITH

graphix

An Imprint of

SCHOLASTIC

New York   Toronto   London   Auckland   Sydney   Mexico City   New Delhi   Hong Kong

All rights reserved. Published by Graphix, an imprint of Scholastic Inc., *Publishers since 1920.*
SCHOLASTIC, GRAPHIX, and associated logos are trademarks and/or registered trademarks of
Scholastic Inc.

ISBN 978-0-545-21142-0

CREDITS

Text for "History of the Valley" written by Jeff Smith

Additional text for "About Jeff Smith," "History of the Valley,"
"The Characters," "A Conversation with Jeff Smith," "How *BONE* Was Colored,"
and "A Conversation with Steve Hamaker" written by Bob Cooper

Harvestar Family Crest designed by Charles Vess

Map of *The Valley* by Mark Crilley

Color by Steve Hamaker

10 9 8 7 6 5 4 3 2 1   10 11 12 13

First edition, February 2010

Edited by Cassandra Pelham

Book design by Phil Falco

Creative Director: David Saylor

Printed in the United States 113

CONTENTS

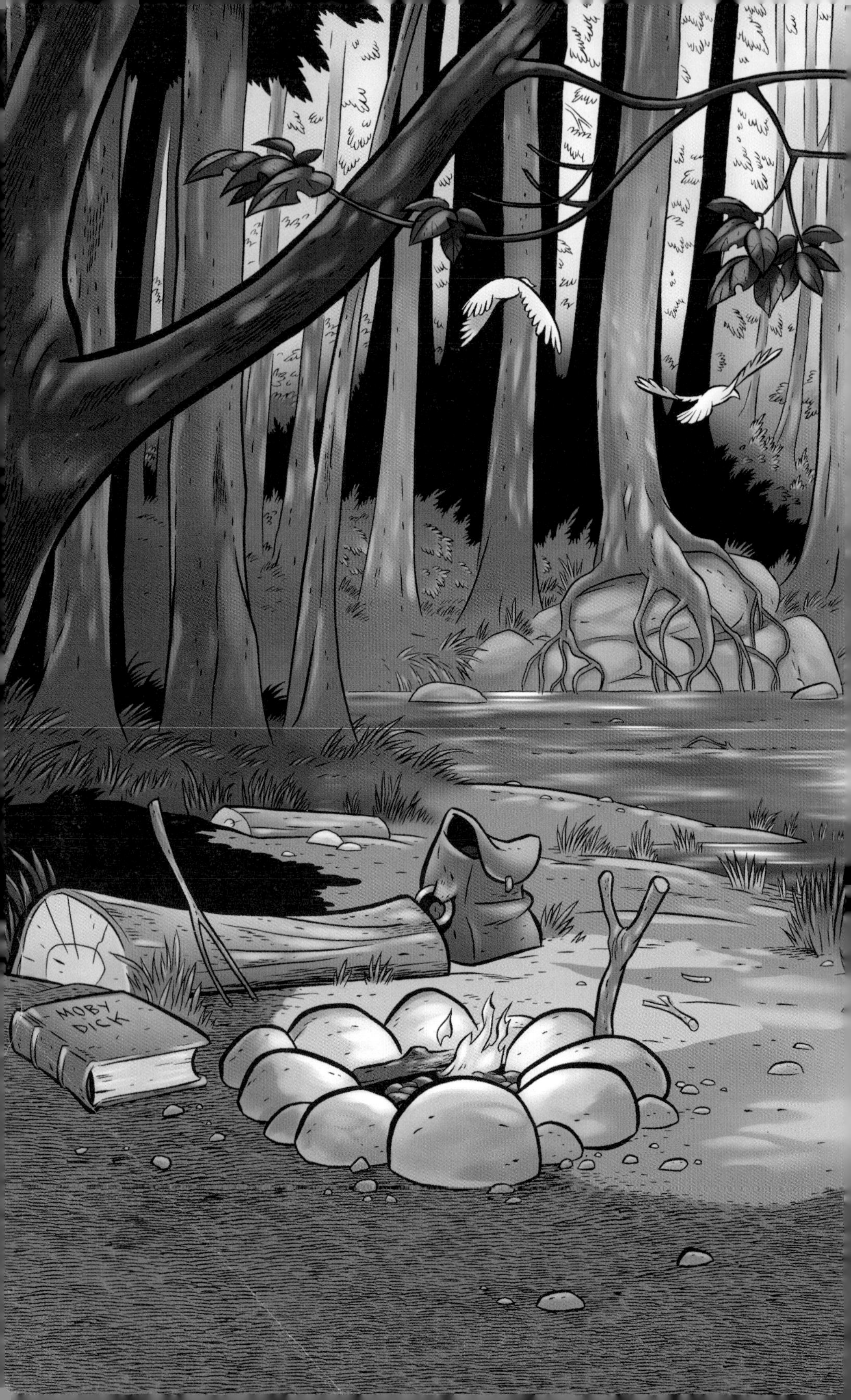
MOBY
DICK

WELCOME TO
THE WORLD OF BONE!

THE EPIC ADVENTURES of Fone Bone, Smiley Bone, and Phoney Bone first appeared in 1991 as a series of black-and-white comic books. Since then, *BONE* has been published in color editions by Scholastic/Graphix and has sold millions of copies around the world.

Inside this book you'll find rare *BONE* comics, cover art from the original editions, a history of the Valley and its mythology, info about your favorite characters, interviews with creator Jeff Smith and colorist Steve Hamaker, a look at how *BONE* was colored, little-known facts about the series, and more!

> **FUN FACT:** Did you know that *BONE* has been published in twenty-five countries, including Finland, Indonesia, and Singapore?

ABOUT JEFF SMITH

Jeff (left), age five, with younger brother Randy.

CARTOONS AND COMICS fascinated Jeff as a child. His favorites were Walt Kelly's *Pogo* and Disney's *Uncle Scrooge*, but he also loved Bugs Bunny, Woody Woodpecker, Mickey Mouse, Donald Duck, and Charlie Brown and the *Peanuts* gang. *The Adventures of Tintin*, a hugely popular comic featuring a boy reporter and his dog, Snowy, was another influence. And later, Jeff enjoyed superheroes such as Batman and Green Lantern – and any other hero drawn by his favorite artist, Neal Adams. It didn't take Jeff long to start drawing his own comics. On family visits to Connecticut, his grandmother would bring home stacks of paper for him to draw on. By the time he was in kindergarten, he was already inventing characters that would eventually find their way into *BONE.* Doodles of these characters kept appearing in the margins of his school assignments and on the covers of his notebooks – they took on a life of their own!

When Jeff was about nine years old, a classmate brought a big book of *Pogo* comic strip reprints to school. Jeff thought *Pogo* was the greatest thing he'd ever seen! But by the seventh grade Jeff had moved on from comic books altogether. Sweeping fantasy epics had begun to inspire him: The Chronicles of Narnia, The Lord of the Rings, and especially the first three Star Wars movies. He was also intrigued by the legend of King Arthur and the riveting Greek classics *The Iliad* and *The Odyssey.* These tales would inspire the *BONE* saga even more than *Pogo* and the other comics he read when he was younger.

FONE-BONE
BY Jeff SMITH
TABLET BOOK #1
CO STARRING:
PHONEY-BONE
THE GEM!

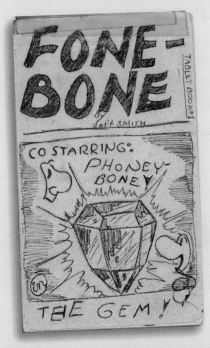

One of the very first *BONE* stories, created by Jeff when he was about ten years old.

FONE BONE!
!
YES SIR!
PUT THIS IN THE VAULT
YES SIR!
HI
ARRGH!
LOOK!
GAK

In high school, one of Jeff's teachers urged him to attend art school, and he received a scholarship to attend the Columbus College of Art & Design. At that time, most art schools didn't take cartooning very seriously, or even consider it a real art form. Before long Jeff transferred to The Ohio State University, where he wrote and drew a daily comic strip for the college newspaper, the *Lantern*, for four years.

The characters in Jeff's *Lantern* strip were early versions of the familiar *BONE* characters – in fact, the title of the strip was *Thorn*. Jeff tried selling the comic strip to the major newspapers, but they turned him down.

After Jeff graduated from college, he cofounded the Character Builders animation studio in Columbus, Ohio, with a couple of friends. Together they worked on everything from public service announcements and commercials to cartoons and major animated films. He was still putting in long hours at the studio when he started working on the first issues of *BONE*.

In 1991, Jeff founded Cartoon Books to publish *BONE*. His wife, Vijaya Iyer, joined the company the next year to guide the business side of things. Publishing and distributing his own *BONE* comic books became a real possibility for the first time.

Did you know that Jeff planned out the entire story arc of what would eventually become the nine-volume *BONE* series before he even began working on the first page? In fact, he drew the last page first! Knowing the ending helped keep Jeff focused on where the story was heading during the more than twelve years it took to complete the series.

FUN FACT: Did you know that *BONE* has won ten Eisner Awards (like the Oscars, but for comics)?

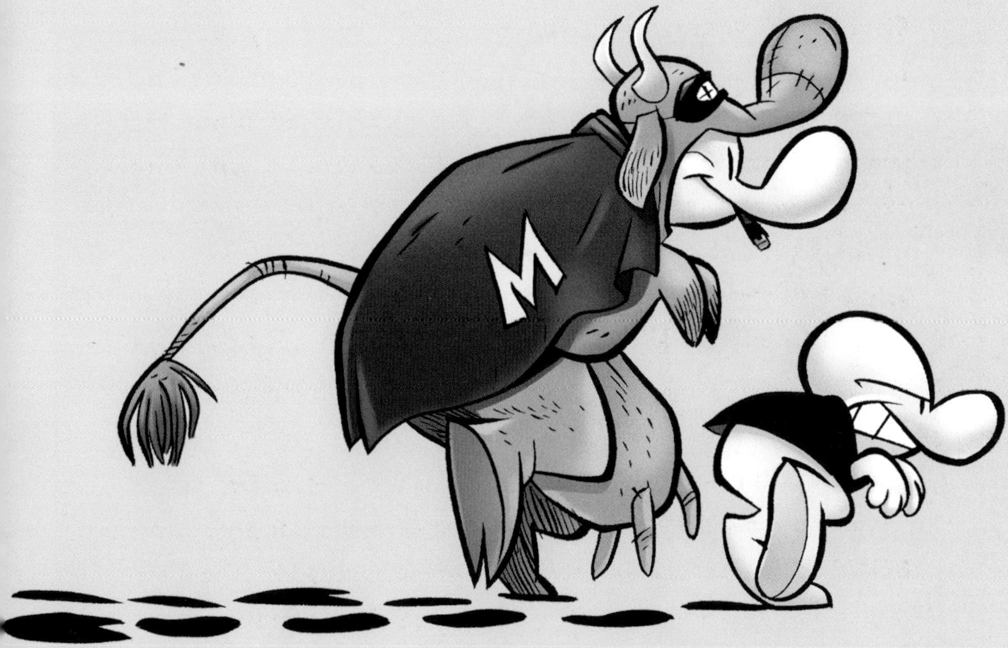

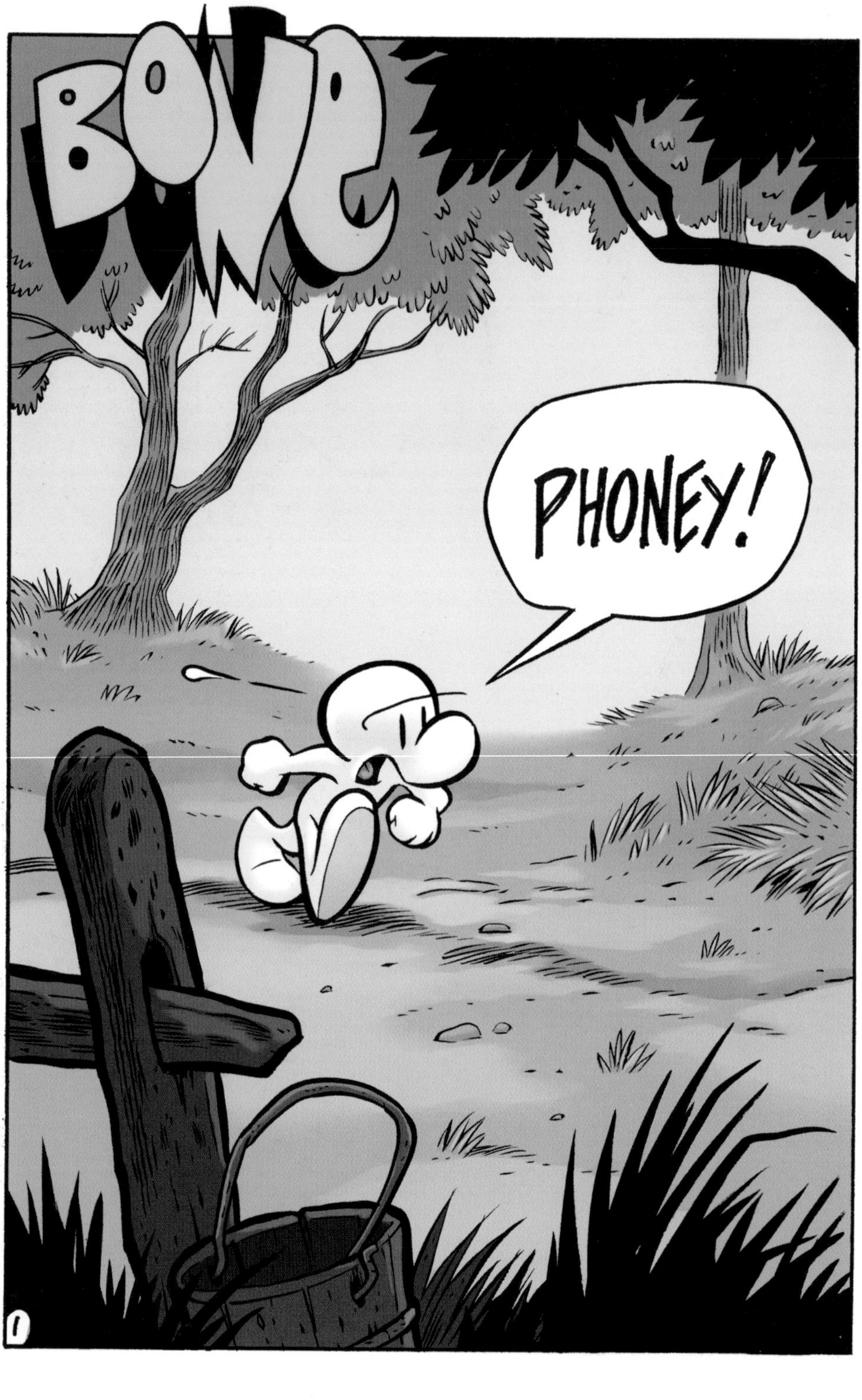
BONE
PHONEY!
1

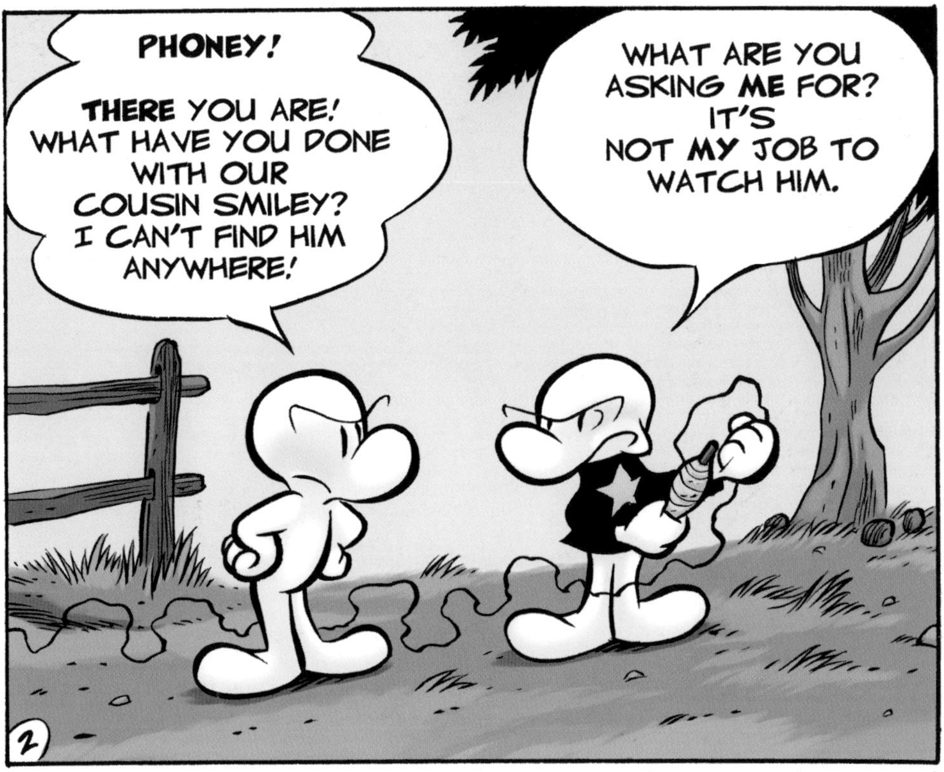
PHONEY! THERE YOU ARE! WHAT HAVE YOU DONE WITH OUR COUSIN SMILEY? I CAN'T FIND HIM ANYWHERE!
WHAT ARE YOU ASKING ME FOR? IT'S NOT MY JOB TO WATCH HIM.
2

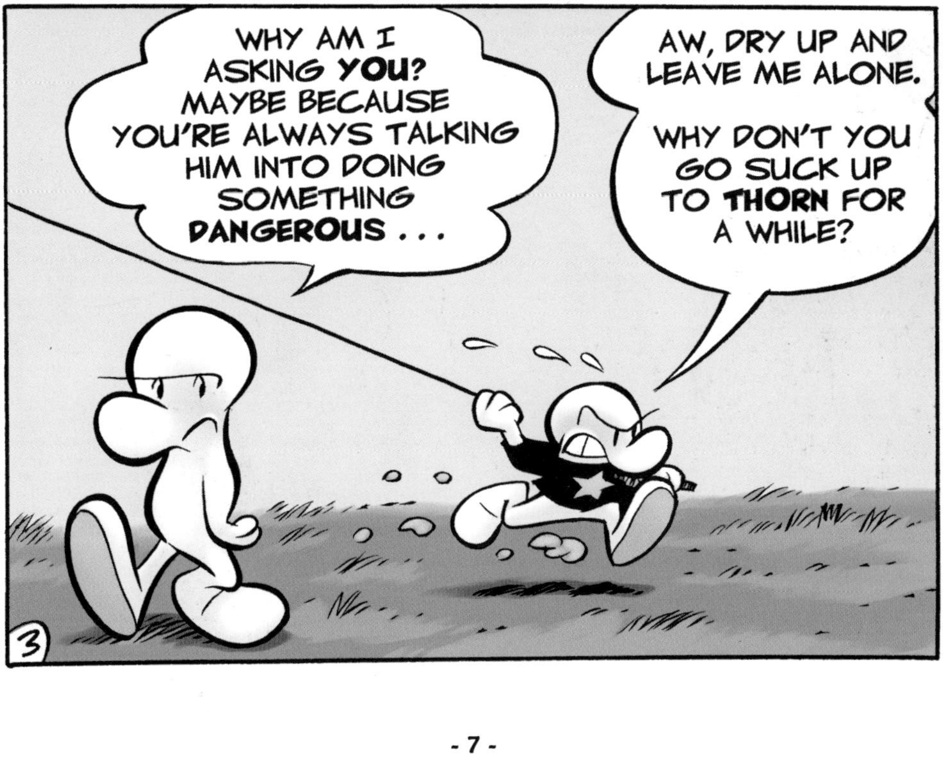
WHY AM I ASKING YOU? MAYBE BECAUSE YOU'RE ALWAYS TALKING HIM INTO DOING SOMETHING DANGEROUS . . .
AW, DRY UP AND LEAVE ME ALONE. WHY DON'T YOU GO SUCK UP TO THORN FOR A WHILE?
3

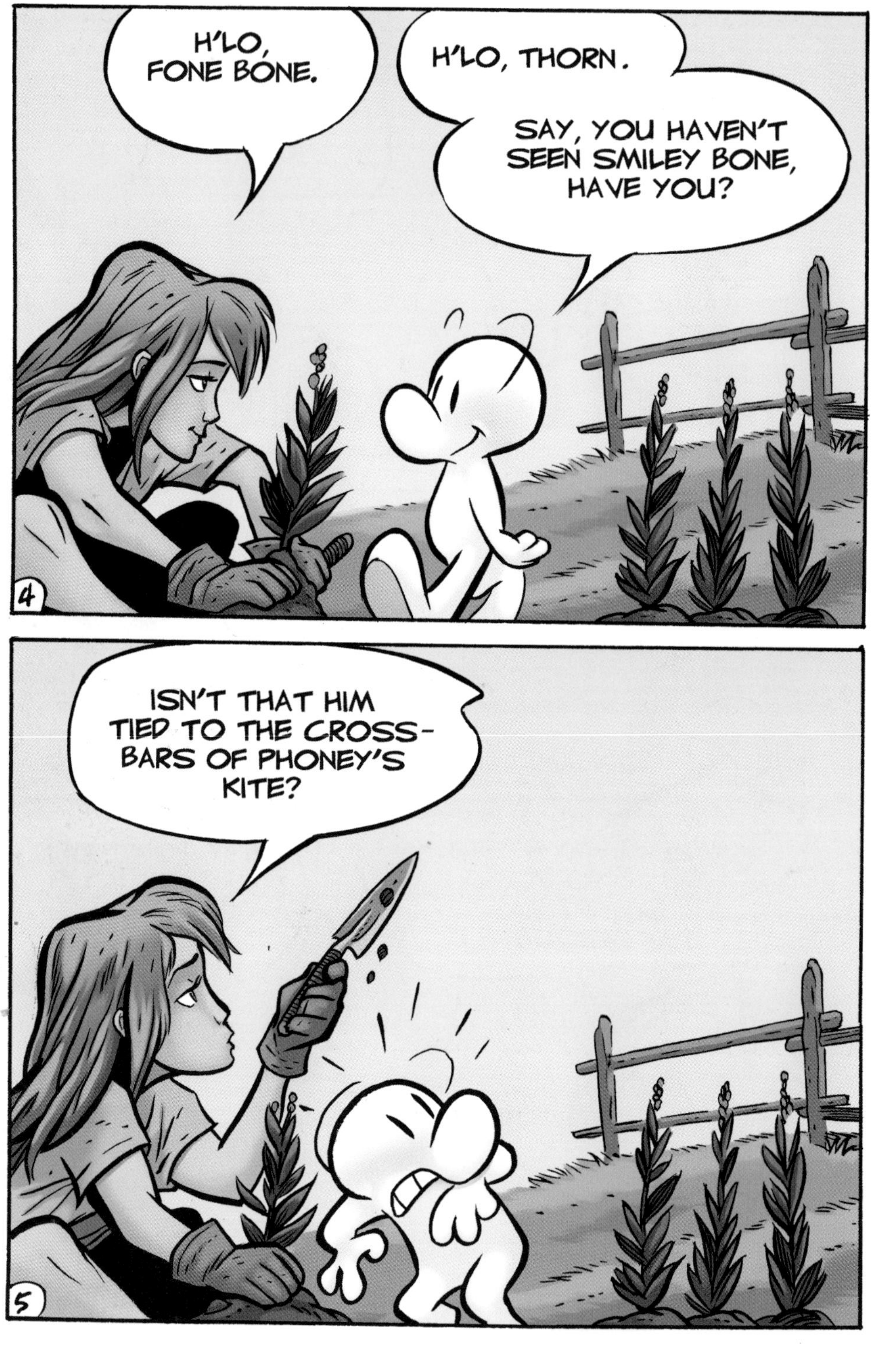
H'LO, FONE BONE.
H'LO, THORN.
SAY, YOU HAVEN'T SEEN SMILEY BONE, HAVE YOU?
4
ISN'T THAT HIM TIED TO THE CROSS-BARS OF PHONEY'S KITE?
5

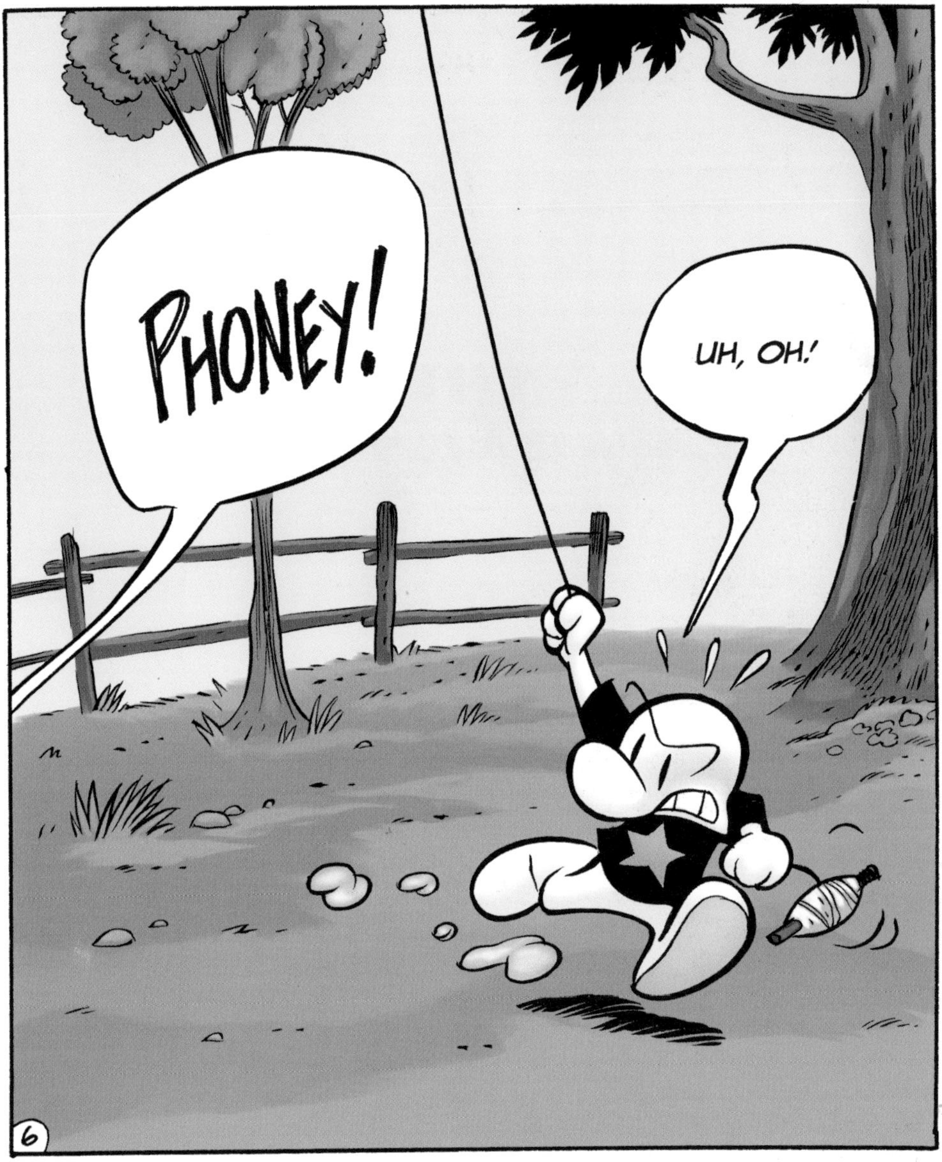
PHONEY!
UH, OH!

To be continued on page 28

THE CHARACTERS

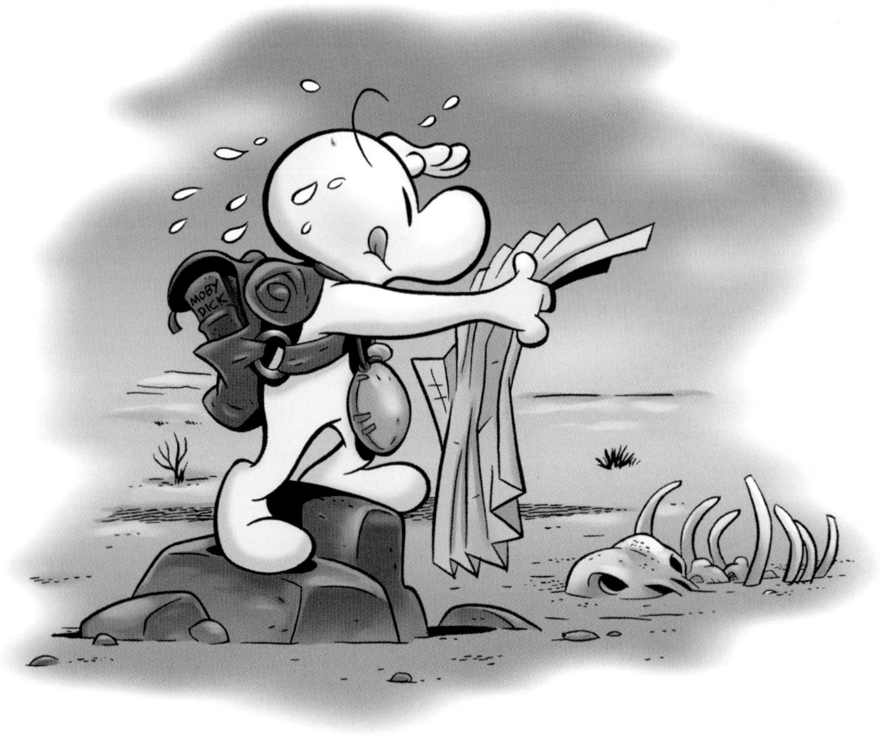
MOBY DICK

FONE BONE

Fone Bone keeps his wits about him in even the most dangerous situations, and because of that he's the bravest of the Bones.

His favorite book is *Moby Dick*, and he'll regale anyone within earshot with a page or two of Herman Melville's classic. But what he really likes more than anything else is Thorn (the love letters prove it!), and they end up becoming the best of friends.

Aside from the Rat Creatures and other enemies the Bones meet in the Valley, there's not much that Fone Bone doesn't like (except maybe Phoney Bone's latest moneymaking scheme).

PHONCIBLE P. (PHONEY) BONE

Phoney Bone is always looking for the quickest and easiest way to get rich. Most of his scams result in disaster (like the one that got the Bone cousins run out of Boneville), but that doesn't stop him from planning his next get-rich-quick scheme.

As the eldest, Phoney raised Fone Bone and Smiley Bone when they were young orphans in Boneville. Because of this, he is resourceful, and despite his mostly greedy and selfish ways, he is very protective of his cousins. Phoney risks his life to defend them – even when the Hooded One is doing the threatening!

SMILEY BONE

Smiley Bone is really, really good at driving everyone around him crazy – especially his two cousins. He has a great heart and a happy-go-lucky attitude, and he's always eager to help Phoney with his outrageous schemes.

As orphans in Boneville, Phoney could convince Smiley to do just about anything, including stealing pies from windowsills (because he was the tallest!). After Phoney got rich, however, Smiley made him pay everyone back for the stolen food. Smiley has a one-string banjo, and he loves a good tune. He likes having no responsibilities because it allows him to be "free as a bird!"

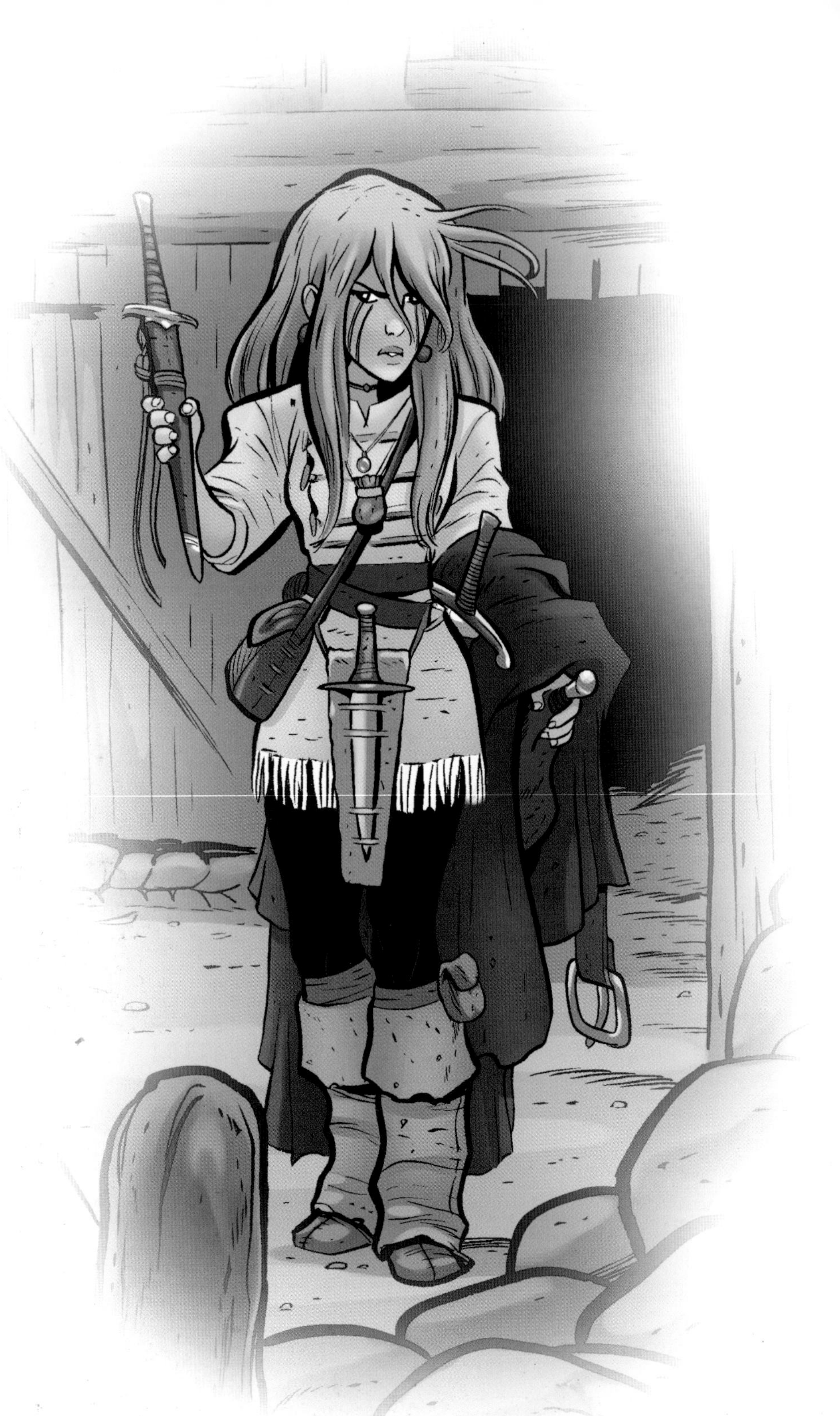

THORN HARVESTAR

Thorn isn't just a farm girl – she's the heir to the throne of Atheia. She's also a Veni Yan Cari, which means she can sense things that others can't and can "see" things in her mind without looking at them. She has great stamina and strength, and even more amazingly, she can fly! She can do pretty much anything simply by concentrating the Dreaming ability that she's inherited. She's courageous in the face of danger – especially when Fone Bone is there to help out.

FUN FACT: Did you know that Jeff Smith's wife, Vijaya, was the inspiration for Thorn?

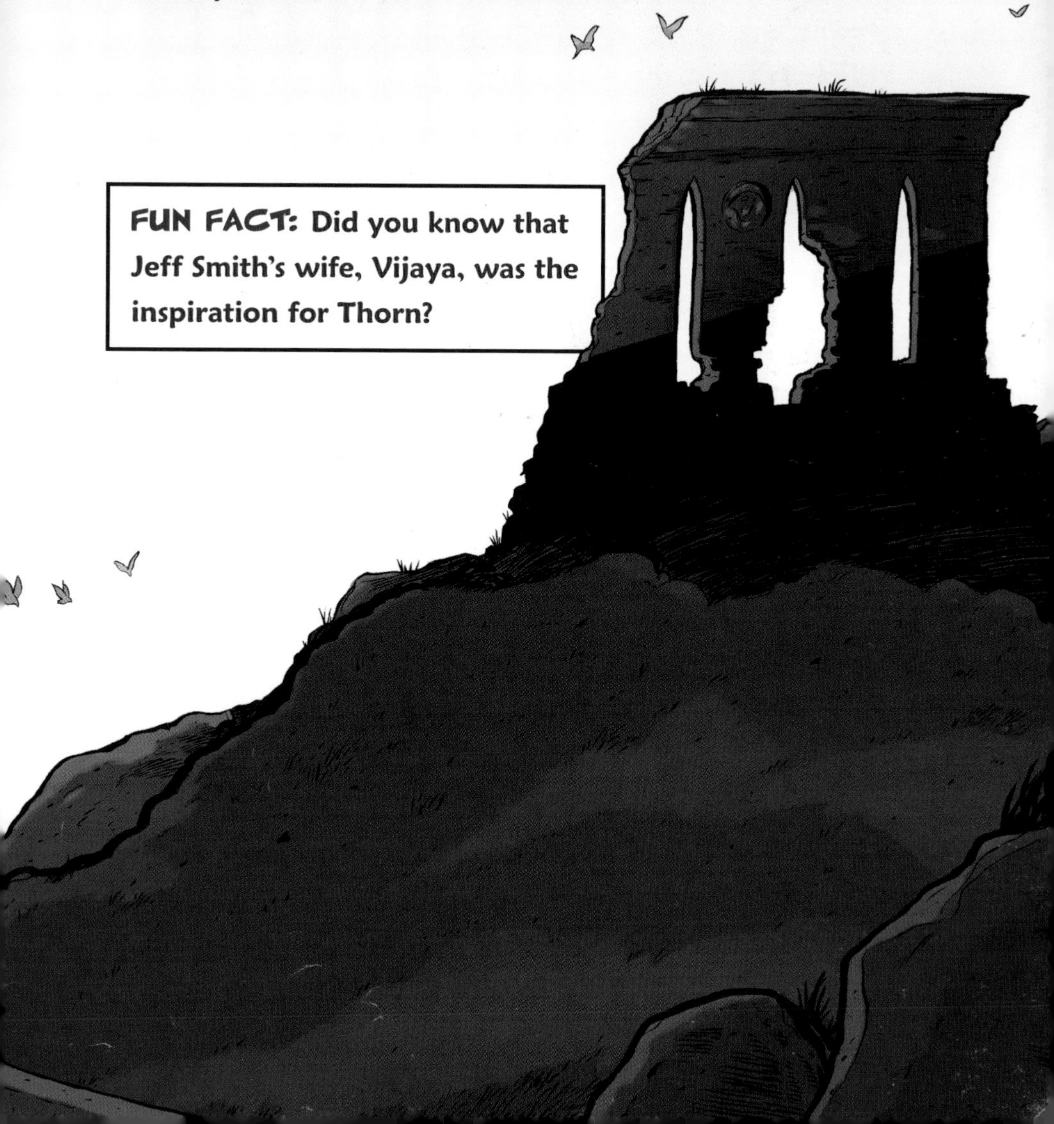

GRAN'MA BEN (ROSE HARVESTAR)

Gran'ma Ben, Thorn's grandmother, is a tough-as-nails farmer ready and willing to take on anyone or anything at a moment's notice. She's amazingly strong, and can fight off packs of Rat Creatures with her bare hands!

Gran'ma Ben has been hiding many secrets. For one, she's actually Queen Rose of Atheia. Following the events that led to Atheia's downfall, Rose escaped to Barrelhaven and raised Thorn while keeping her ignorant of her heritage.

She loves cows, and one of her favorite hobbies is racing them. She's the undefeated champion of the Great Cow Race, the main event of Barrelhaven's annual Spring Fair, and folks come from miles around to cheer her on. In fact, she claims that despite her age, there's still not a cow in the Valley that can outrun her!

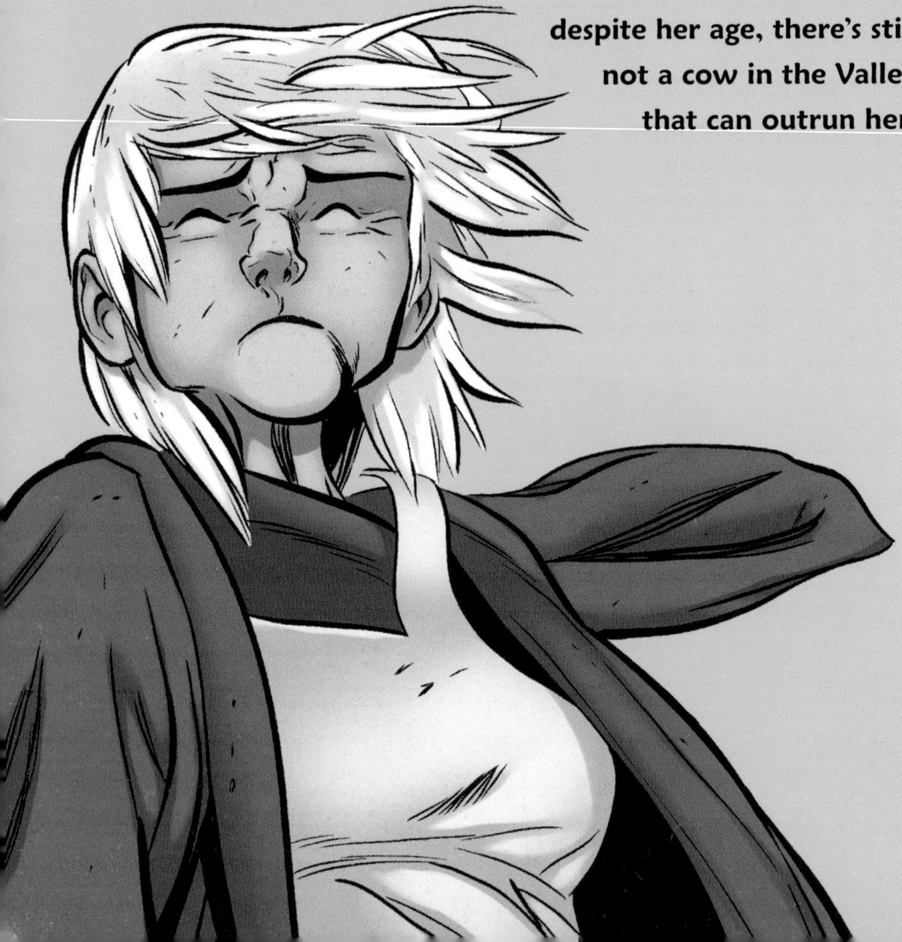

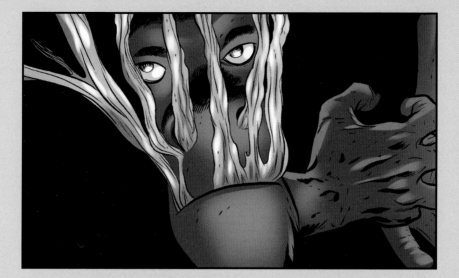

THE GREAT RED DRAGON

The Great Red Dragon is the son of Mim. He becomes Fone Bone's protector of sorts, always mysteriously appearing at the last minute to save him from the Rat Creatures and other threats. The Red Dragon kept an eye on young Thorn during the Great War while Gran'ma Ben searched for a good hiding place. Sometime in the past, however, the Red Dragon seems to have let Gran'ma Ben down. She says of him, "You think th' Dragon'll be there whenever you need him. . . . Well, he won't be."

FUN FACT: Did you know that the Red Dragon is based on a dog named **Commander** that Jeff Smith had when he was younger?

LUCIUS DOWN

Lucius is nearly seven feet tall, weighs almost three hundred pounds, and is the owner of the Barrelhaven Tavern. He's devoted to his customers and a hard taskmaster to his employees, and he loves a good mug of ale every once in a while.

Phoney's arrival in Barrelhaven instantly rubs Lucius the wrong way. Phoney is determined to control Barrelhaven, but Lucius outwits Phoney every time!

Lucius has a long history with Gran'ma Ben. Everyone in the Valley knows of his affection for her, but no one really knows how deeply their history runs.

> **FUN FACT:** Did you know that the Bone cousins were called "Bones" by creator Jeff Smith because he thought they looked like cartoon dog bones?

BARTLEBY

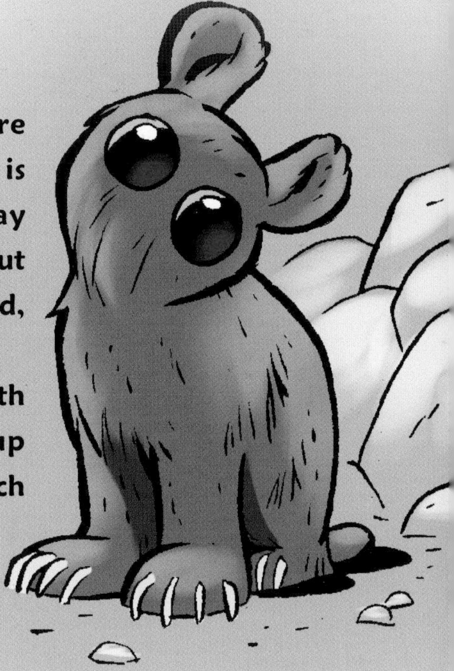

Bartleby is a friendly Rat Creature cub who deserts the horde and is found by the Bones. He ran away after getting his tail chopped off but before he could get his ears cropped, as all Rat Creatures do.

Bartleby has a special bond with Smiley Bone and never passes up the chance to have a blank sandwich with him!

TED THE BUG

Ted pops up in the story from time to time. He's the first creature that Fone Bone meets in the Valley, and the two become fast friends. But don't mistake Ted for a leaf, or he might get his big – and we do mean BIG – brother to clear up your confusion!

There's a lot more to Ted than meets the eye. He's a reliable friend and always has the latest Valley gossip. He also has a mysterious link to the Red Dragon and some power of his own. Ted doesn't like being talked down to and proudly claims, "Bugs know a lotta stuff folks wouldn't s'pose they'd know."

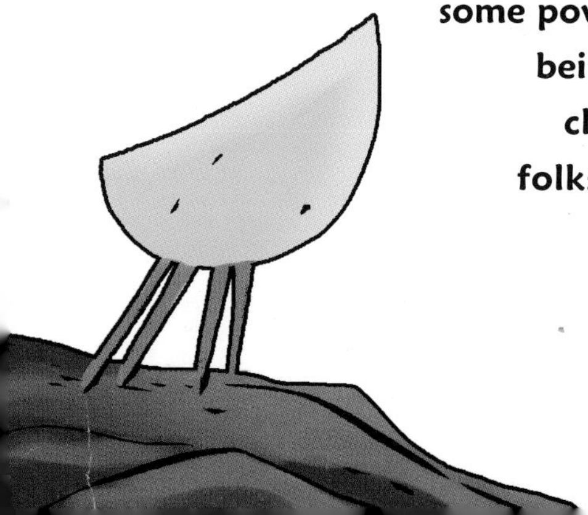

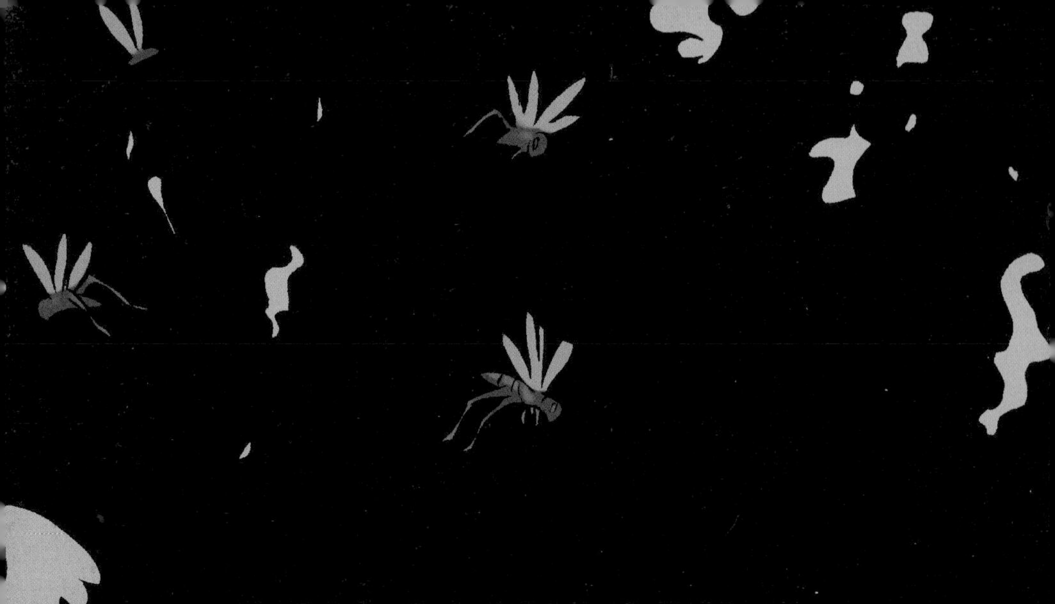

LORD OF THE LOCUSTS

The Lord of the Locusts lurks behind the scenes throughout most of the story, and he commands the Hooded One to do his bidding. In much earlier times, he entered and possessed the mind of Mim, the first queen of the dragons, who was turned to stone in order to trap the Lord of the Locusts inside her.

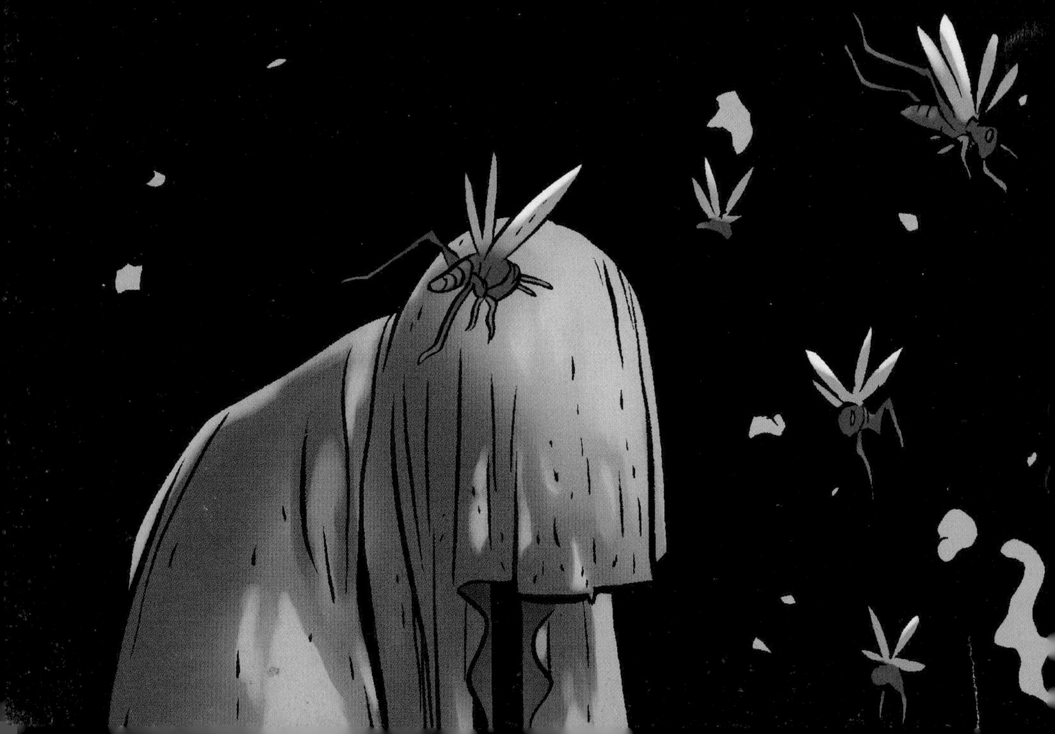

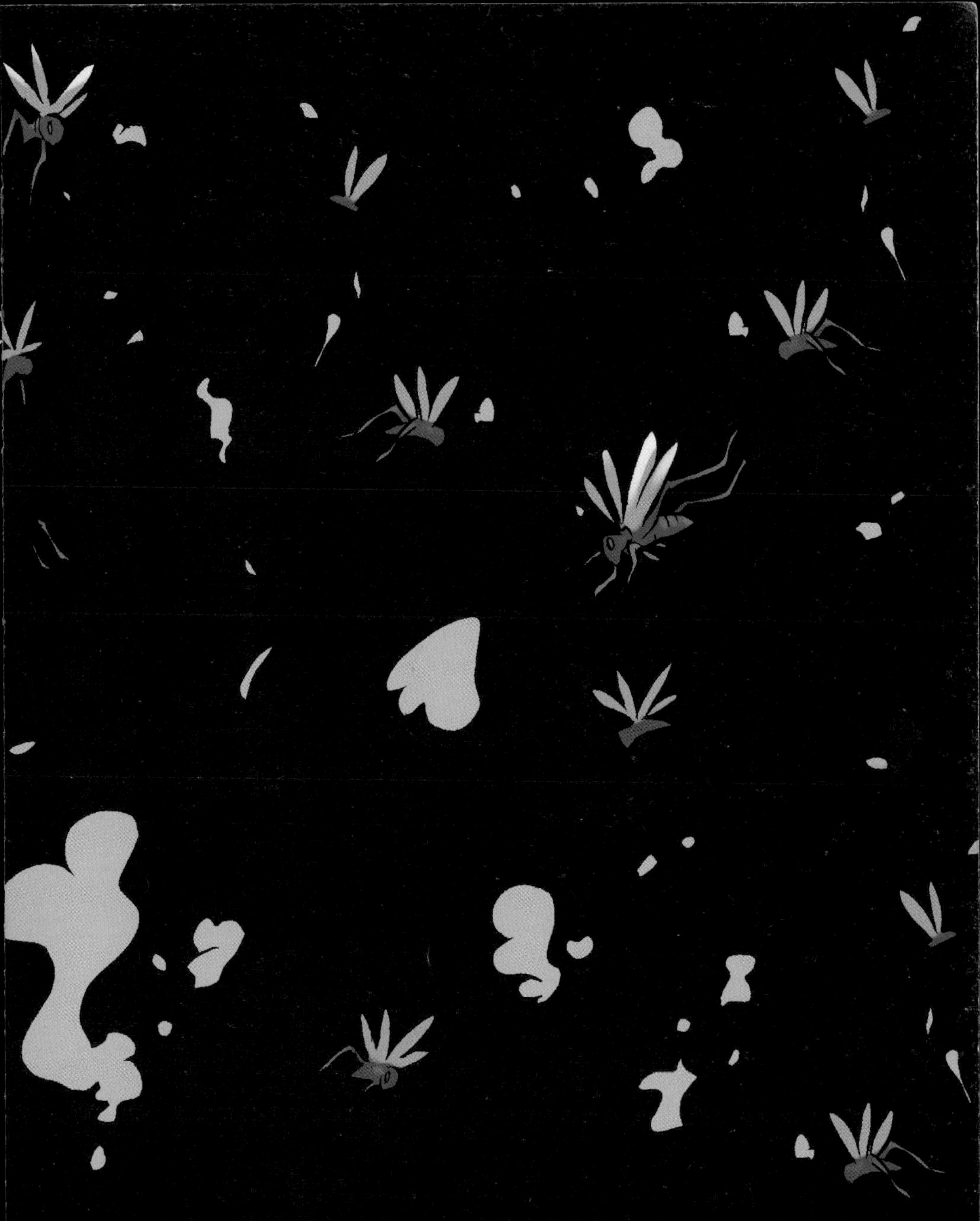

THE HOODED ONE (BRIAR HARVESTAR)

The Hooded One, who is actually Gran'ma Ben's older sister, Briar, serves the Lord of the Locusts and has control over Kingdok and the rat creatures.

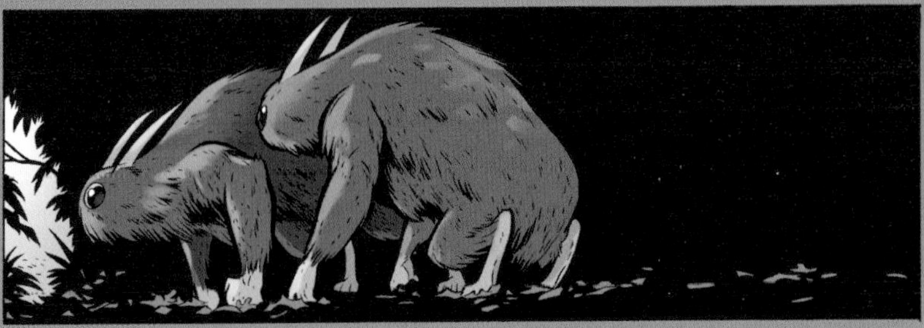

RAT CREATURES

The Rat Creatures, called the "Hairy Men" by the people of the Valley, have huge appetites for small, dead animals or just about anything, really, including Bones. Although they're strong and weigh about five hundred pounds each, the Rat Creatures tend to be pretty stupid. They enjoy eating, sleeping, and not much else.

The Bone cousins meet two stupid Rat Creatures who would love to eat them. While one always fantasizes about baking the Bones into a quiche, the other would much prefer to cook them in a stew.

KINGDOK

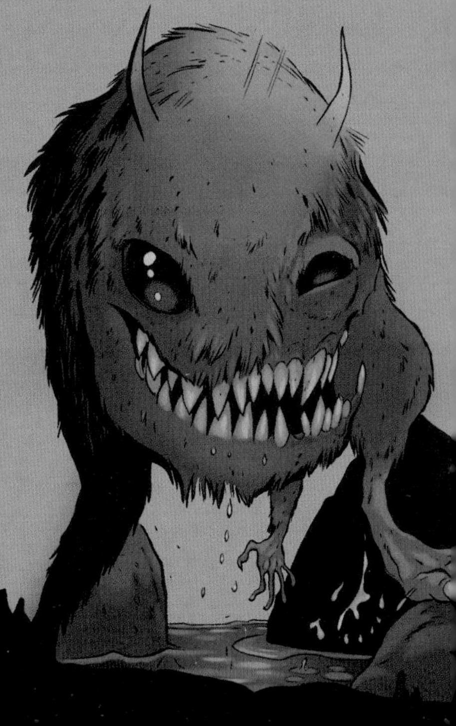

Kingdok is the giant chieftain of the Rat Creatures, who walks on two legs instead of four. He is a longtime enemy of the Atheian royal family and serves the Lord of the Locusts. Kingdok eventually grows tired of being the Hooded One's puppet, but his loyalty to her early on seals his fate.

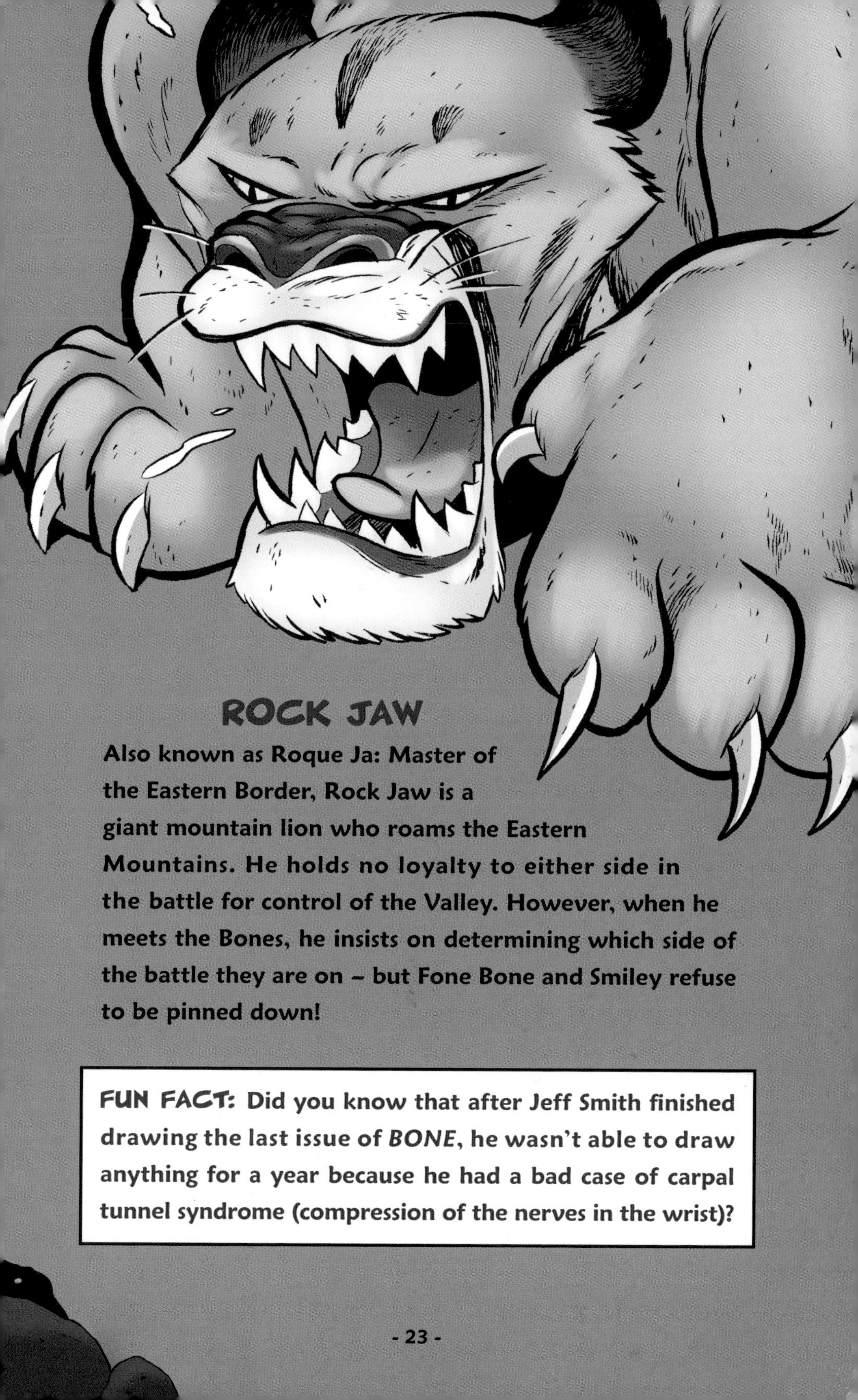

ROCK JAW

Also known as Roque Ja: Master of the Eastern Border, Rock Jaw is a giant mountain lion who roams the Eastern Mountains. He holds no loyalty to either side in the battle for control of the Valley. However, when he meets the Bones, he insists on determining which side of the battle they are on – but Fone Bone and Smiley refuse to be pinned down!

FUN FACT: Did you know that after Jeff Smith finished drawing the last issue of *BONE*, he wasn't able to draw anything for a year because he had a bad case of carpal tunnel syndrome (compression of the nerves in the wrist)?

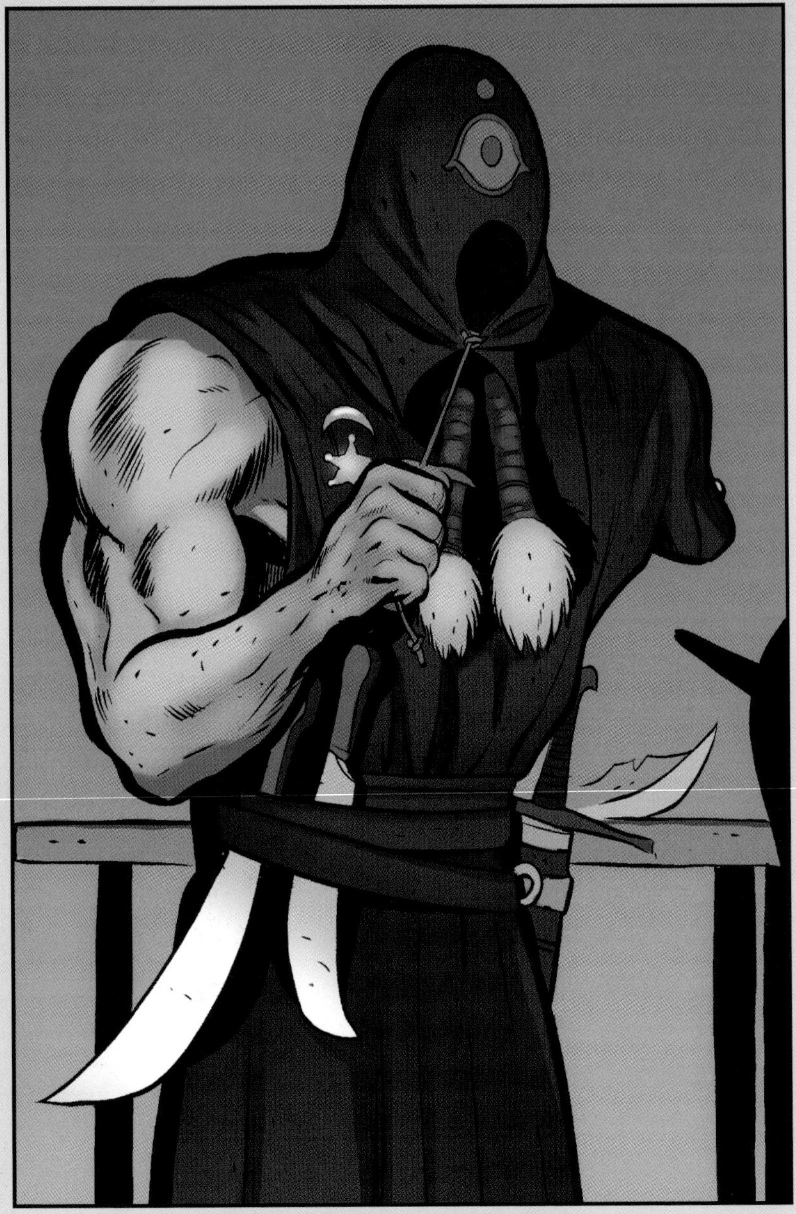

LORD TARSIL

Lord Tarsil is the leader of the Vedu in Atheia and, as such, is the ruler of Atheia at the time that Gran'ma Ben, Thorn, the Bone cousins, and Bartleby arrive in the city.

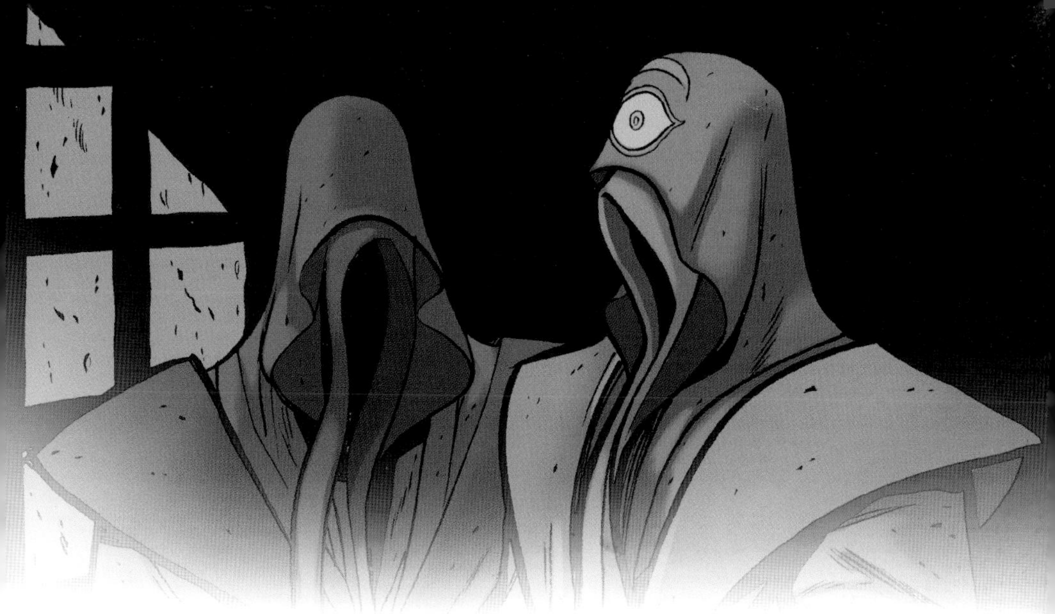

THE VEDU

Also known as the Order of the Dreaming Eye, they are an offshoot of the Veni Yan (see page 45). They only accept the teachings of Ven, the first human queen, and have outlawed Dragon lore.

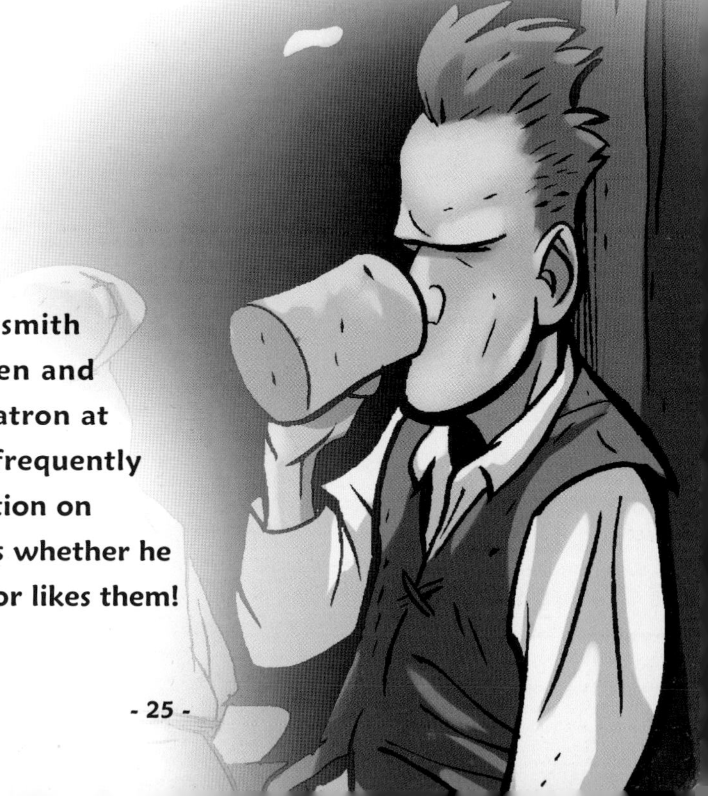

WENDELL

Wendell is a tinsmith from Barrelhaven and an outspoken patron at the Tavern. He frequently changes his position on matters – such as whether he hates the Bones or likes them!

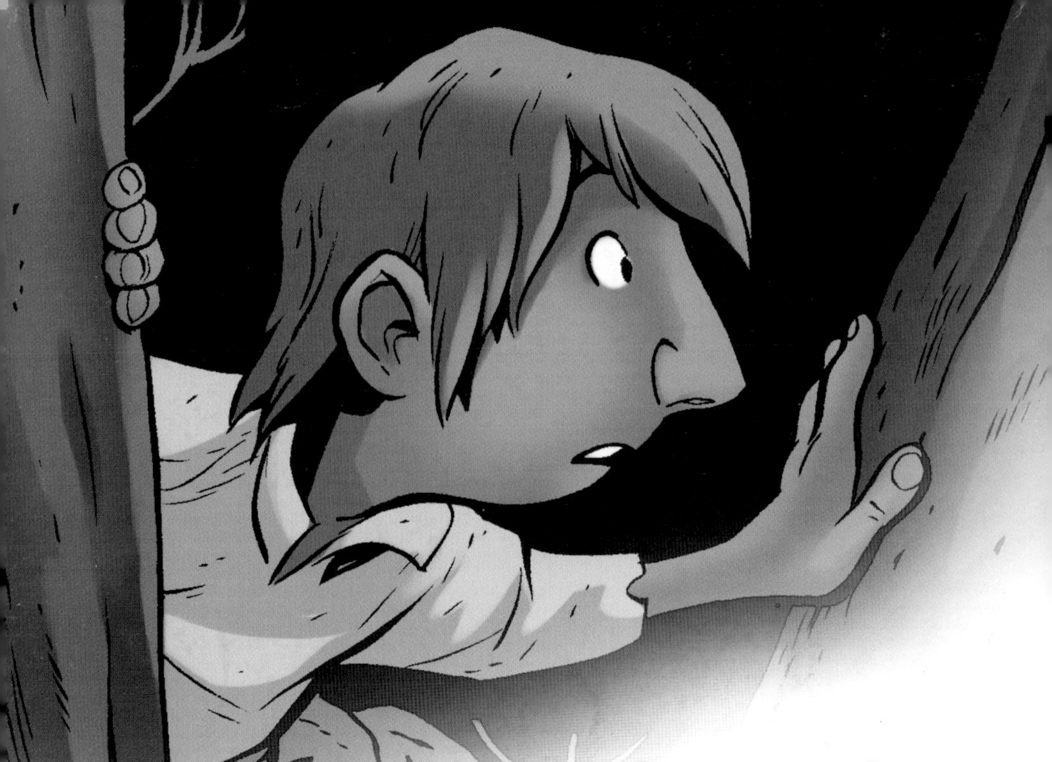

JONATHAN OAKS

Jonathan works for Lucius at the Barrelhaven Tavern and considers him a hero. Despite being small, Jonathan has no problem getting into the mix of things!

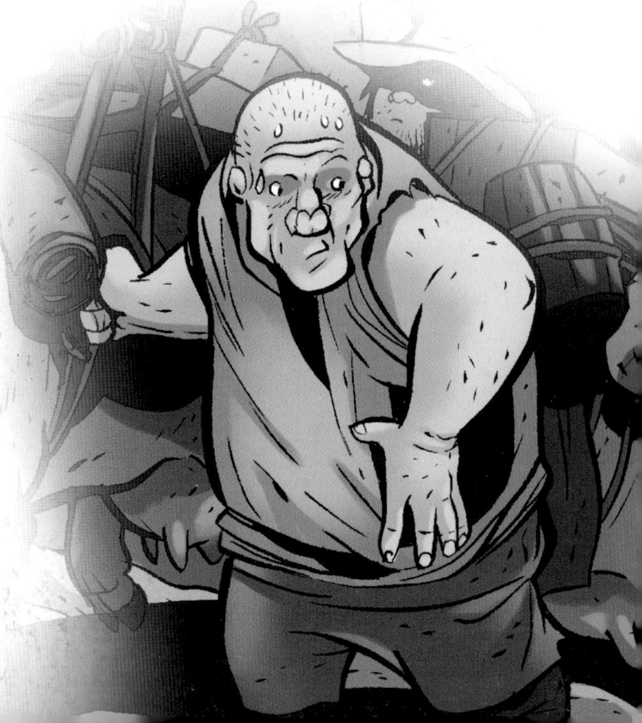

EUCLID

Euclid is Wendell's best friend. He resorts to physical force to solve most problems!

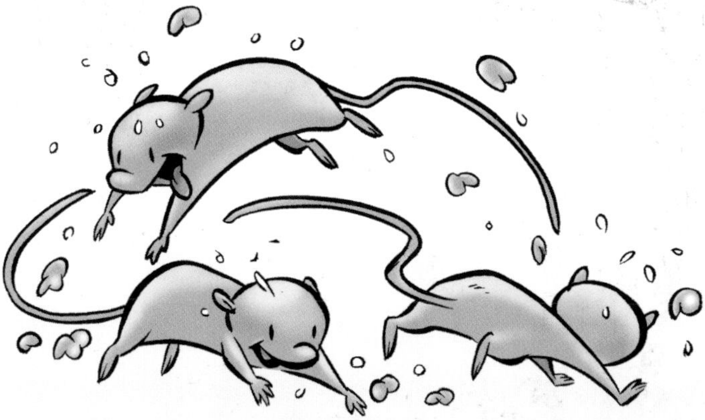

THE POSSUM KIDS

The Possum Kids love adventure and have a way of always finding trouble!

MIZ POSSUM

Miz Possum has her hands full keeping her kids in line, and she also helps Fone Bone during his first winter in the Valley.

TANEAL AND HER BROTHER

Taneal and her brother help Gran'ma Ben, Thorn, and the Bones while they're in Atheia. Taneal has a special knowledge of prayer stones, and she builds the sculpture of Fone Bone and Bartleby that sits in Queen's Square.

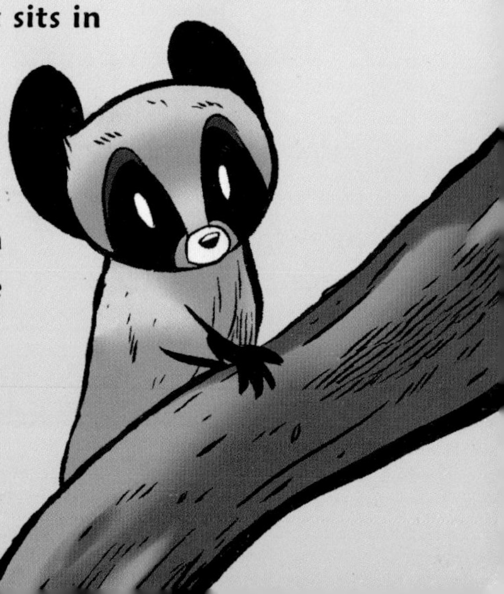

RODERICK

Roderick is an orphaned raccoon whose parents were killed by the two stupid Rat Creatures.

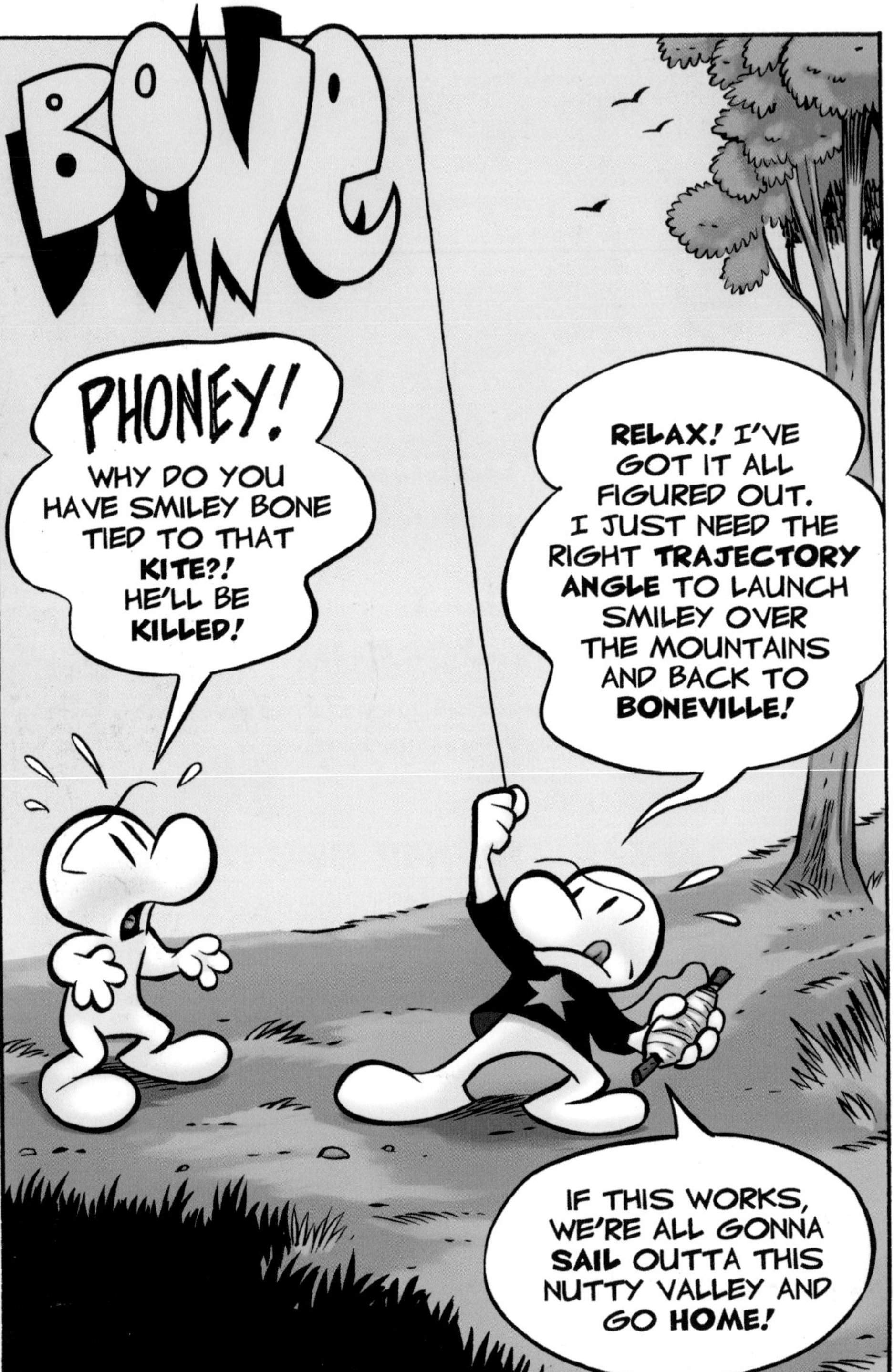
BONE
PHONEY! WHY DO YOU HAVE SMILEY BONE TIED TO THAT KITE?! HE'LL BE KILLED!
RELAX! I'VE GOT IT ALL FIGURED OUT. I JUST NEED THE RIGHT TRAJECTORY ANGLE TO LAUNCH SMILEY OVER THE MOUNTAINS AND BACK TO BONEVILLE!
IF THIS WORKS, WE'RE ALL GONNA SAIL OUTTA THIS NUTTY VALLEY AND GO HOME!
1

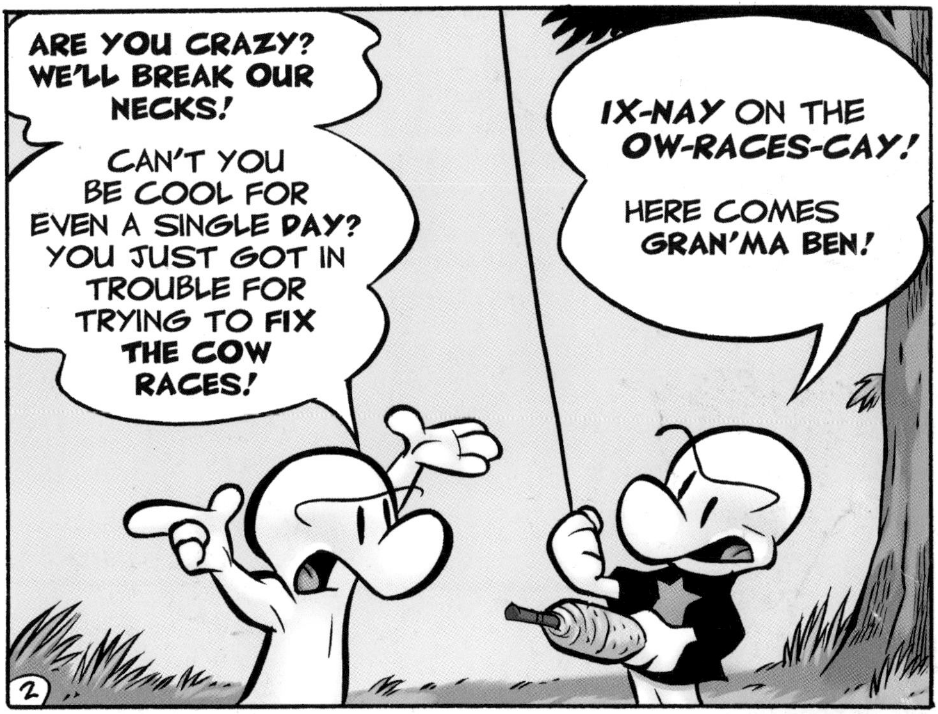
ARE YOU CRAZY? WE'LL BREAK OUR NECKS!
CAN'T YOU BE COOL FOR EVEN A SINGLE DAY? YOU JUST GOT IN TROUBLE FOR TRYING TO FIX THE COW RACES!
IX-NAY ON THE OW-RACES-CAY!
HERE COMES GRAN'MA BEN!
2

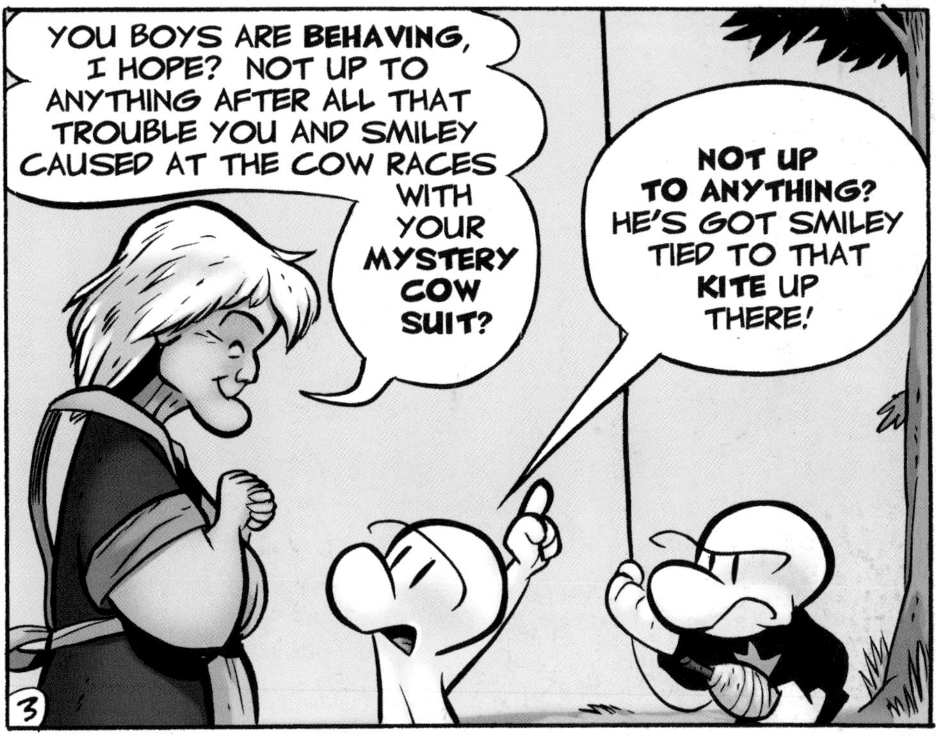
YOU BOYS ARE BEHAVING, I HOPE? NOT UP TO ANYTHING AFTER ALL THAT TROUBLE YOU AND SMILEY CAUSED AT THE COW RACES WITH YOUR MYSTERY COW SUIT?
NOT UP TO ANYTHING? HE'S GOT SMILEY TIED TO THAT KITE UP THERE!
3

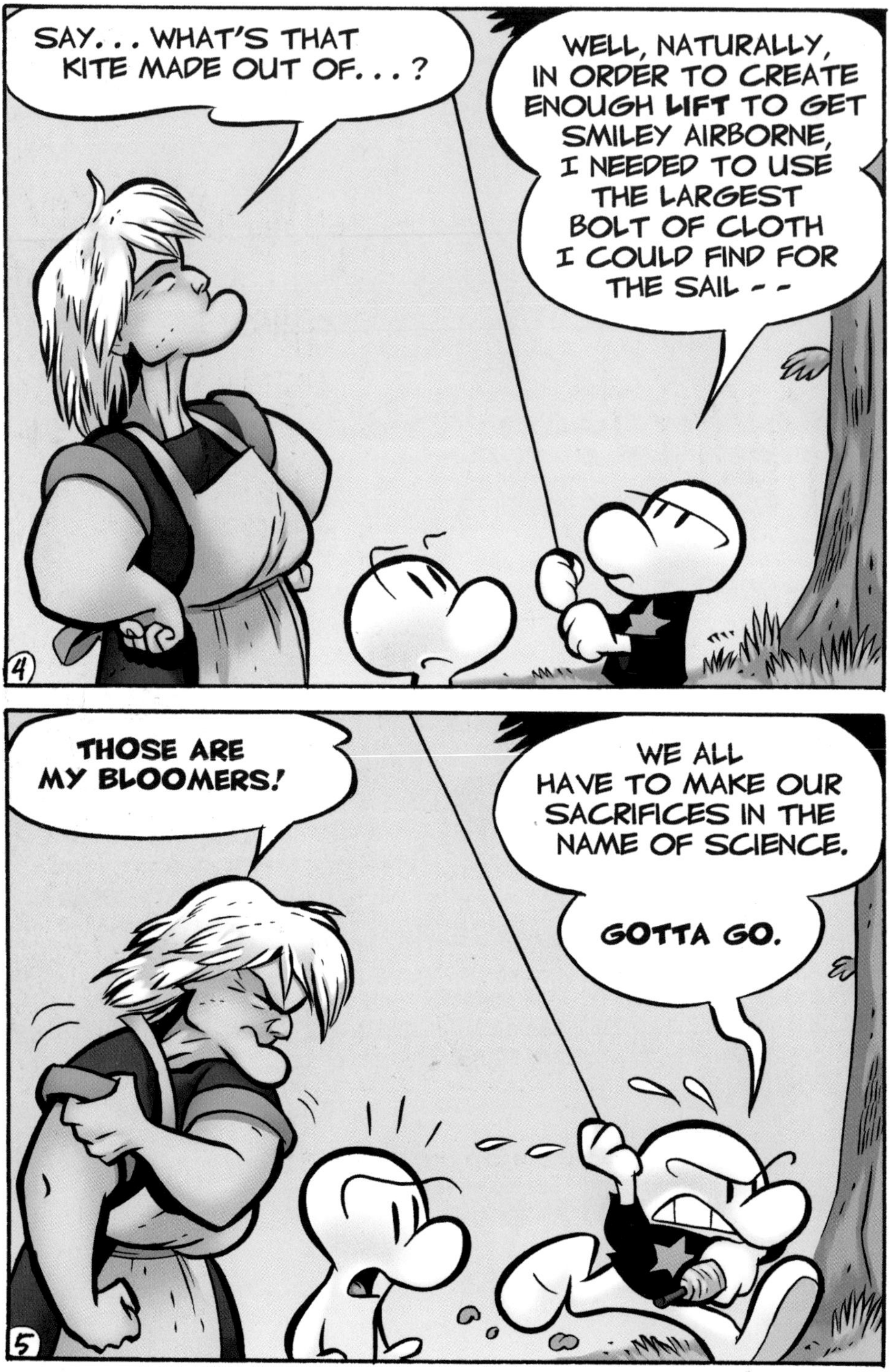
SAY... WHAT'S THAT KITE MADE OUT OF...?
WELL, NATURALLY, IN ORDER TO CREATE ENOUGH **LIFT** TO GET SMILEY AIRBORNE, I NEEDED TO USE THE LARGEST BOLT OF CLOTH I COULD FIND FOR THE SAIL --
THOSE ARE MY BLOOMERS!
WE ALL HAVE TO MAKE OUR SACRIFICES IN THE NAME OF SCIENCE.
GOTTA GO.

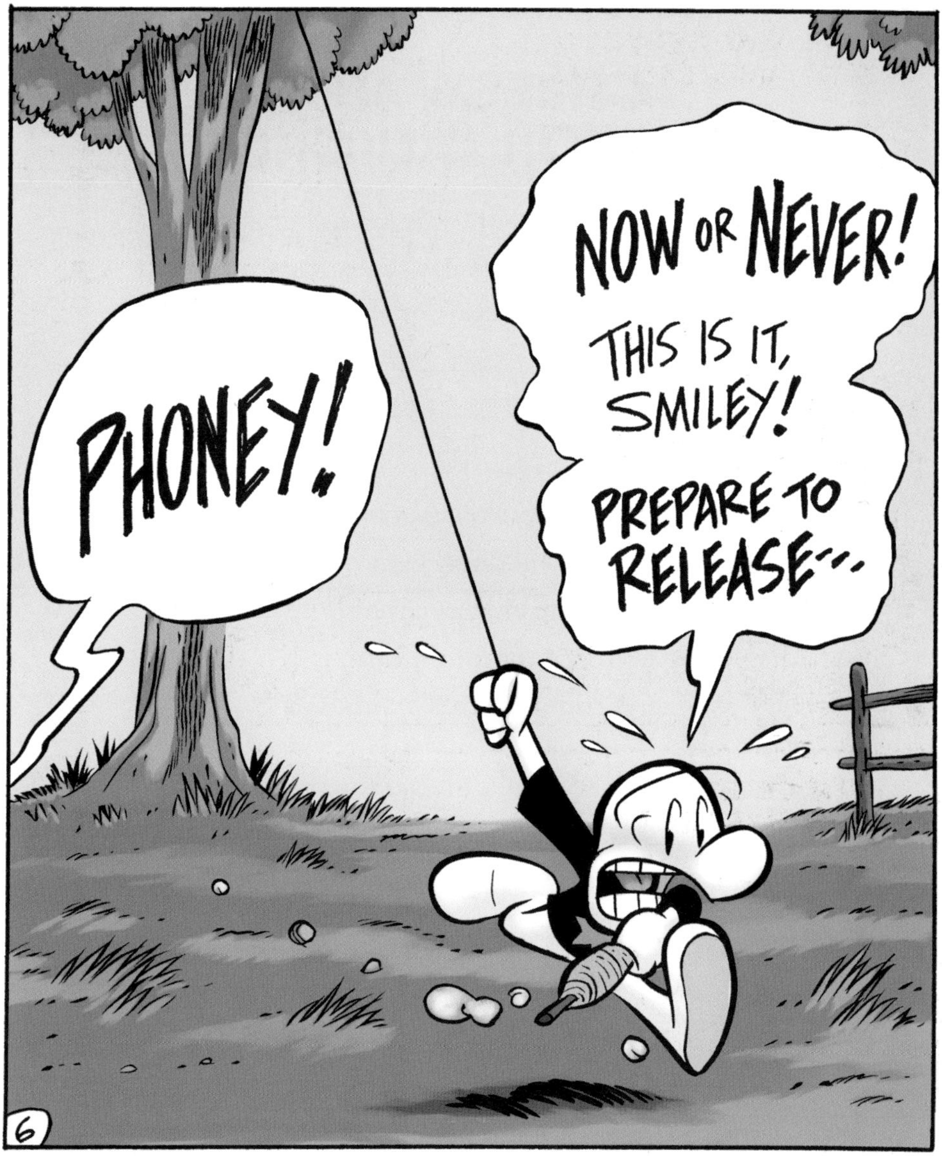
PHONEY!
NOW OR NEVER!
THIS IS IT, SMILEY!
PREPARE TO RELEASE...

To be continued on page 36

CHEESE AND BACON QUICHE

In *Crown of Horns*, Smiley Bone bakes a quiche for the stupid, stupid Rat Creatures. And with adult supervision, you can make one, too!

INGREDIENTS

1 pie crust (prepared or homemade)

1/4 cup butter (softened)

4 medium eggs

2 cups heavy cream

1/2 teaspoon salt

1/2 cup grated Swiss cheese

1 tablespoon butter
(as a separate measurement)

3/4 cup chopped cooked bacon

2 tablespoons minced green onion

1/4 teaspoon salt
(as a separate measurement)

pinch of pepper

dab of soft stinky cheese
(Stilton or Camembert will work)

PREPARATION INSTRUCTIONS

1. Preheat oven to 425°F.

2. Spread 1/4 cup of butter onto the pie crust evenly, then chill.

3. In a large bowl, beat the eggs, heavy cream, and 1/2 teaspoon of salt with a whisk. Stir in the grated cheese.

4. Melt the tablespoon of butter in a skillet over medium-high heat.

5. Add the chopped bacon, minced green onions, 1/4 teaspoon of salt, and pinch of pepper. Cook for 5 minutes or until the onions are tender, stirring frequently.

6. Stir the bacon and onion mixture into the cream mixture.

7. Pour into the pie crust and bake for 15 minutes at 425°F.

8. Reduce heat to 325°F and bake for another 35 minutes.

9. Allow to stand for 10 to 15 minutes.

10. Spoon a dab of soft stinky cheese on top before serving piping hot!

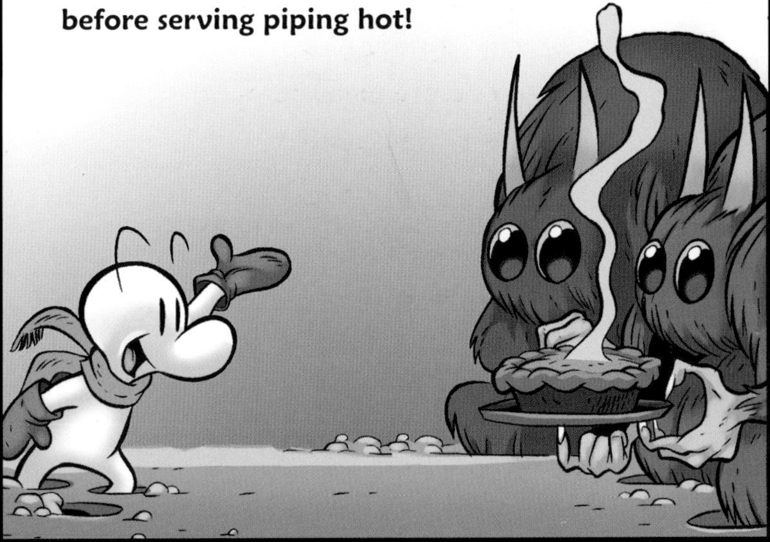

BLANK
SANDWICH

One of Smiley and Bartleby's favorite meals to eat together is a blank sandwich, which is really easy to make!

INGREDIENTS

2 slices of bread

PREPARATION INSTRUCTIONS

1. Remove the crust from each slice of bread.

2. Put the two slices together, cut the sandwich in half, and serve!

PEANUT BUTTER AND PICKLE SANDWICH

Speaking of sandwiches, one of Jeff Smith's favorites has peanut butter and pickles on it. Try one!

INGREDIENTS

2 slices of bread

peanut butter, smooth or chunky

2 dill pickle spears

PREPARATION INSTRUCTIONS

1. Spread a layer of peanut butter on each slice of bread.

2. Carefully cut each pickle spear lengthwise so you have four sections of pickle.

3. Place all four sections on one slice of bread.

4. Lay the other slice of bread on top, and cut the sandwich in half across all four pickle slices.

5. MMM, MMMM! Enjoy with a glass of milk!

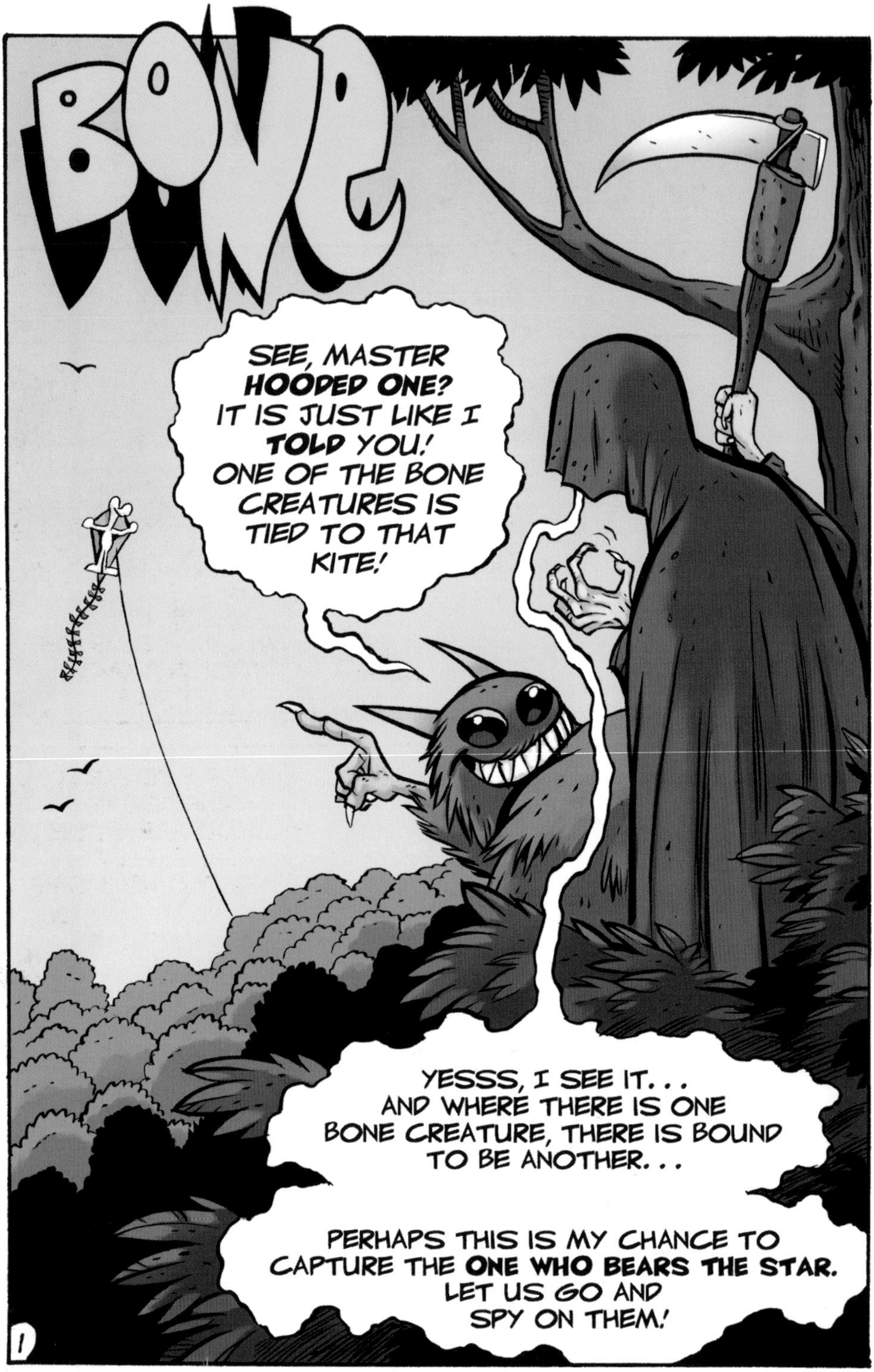
BONE
SEE, MASTER HOODED ONE? IT IS JUST LIKE I TOLD YOU! ONE OF THE BONE CREATURES IS TIED TO THAT KITE!
YESSS, I SEE IT. . . AND WHERE THERE IS ONE BONE CREATURE, THERE IS BOUND TO BE ANOTHER. . .
PERHAPS THIS IS MY CHANCE TO CAPTURE THE ONE WHO BEARS THE STAR. LET US GO AND SPY ON THEM!
1

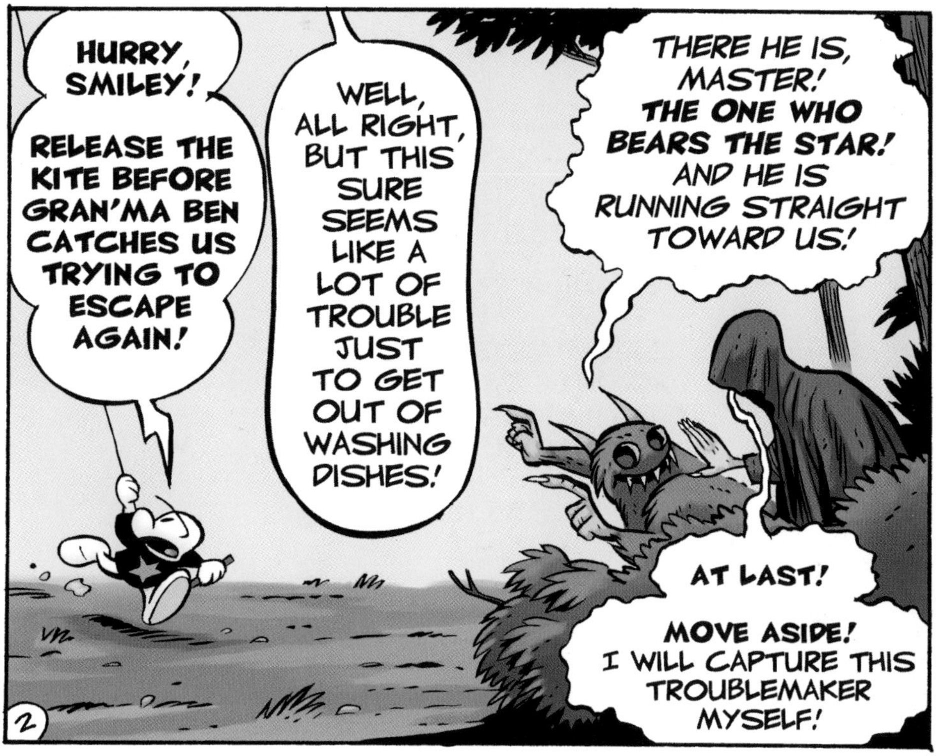
HURRY, SMILEY!
RELEASE THE KITE BEFORE GRAN'MA BEN CATCHES US TRYING TO ESCAPE AGAIN!
WELL, ALL RIGHT, BUT THIS SURE SEEMS LIKE A LOT OF TROUBLE JUST TO GET OUT OF WASHING DISHES!
THERE HE IS, MASTER! THE ONE WHO BEARS THE STAR! AND HE IS RUNNING STRAIGHT TOWARD US!
AT LAST!
MOVE ASIDE! I WILL CAPTURE THIS TROUBLEMAKER MYSELF!
2

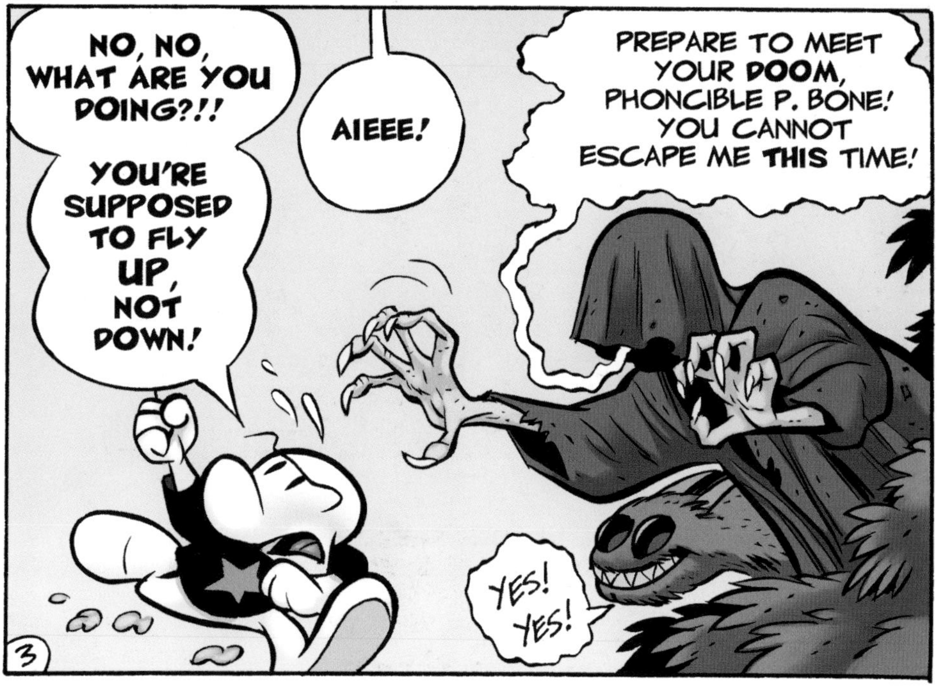
NO, NO, WHAT ARE YOU DOING?!!
YOU'RE SUPPOSED TO FLY UP, NOT DOWN!
AIEEE!
PREPARE TO MEET YOUR DOOM, PHONCIBLE P. BONE! YOU CANNOT ESCAPE ME THIS TIME!
YES! YES!
3

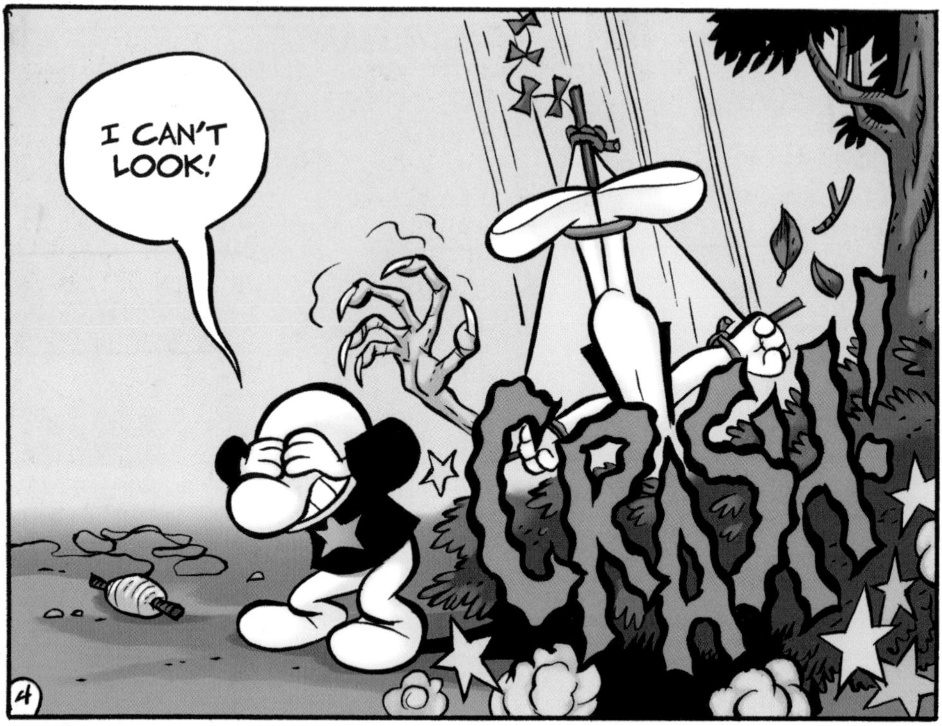
I CAN'T LOOK!
CRASH!

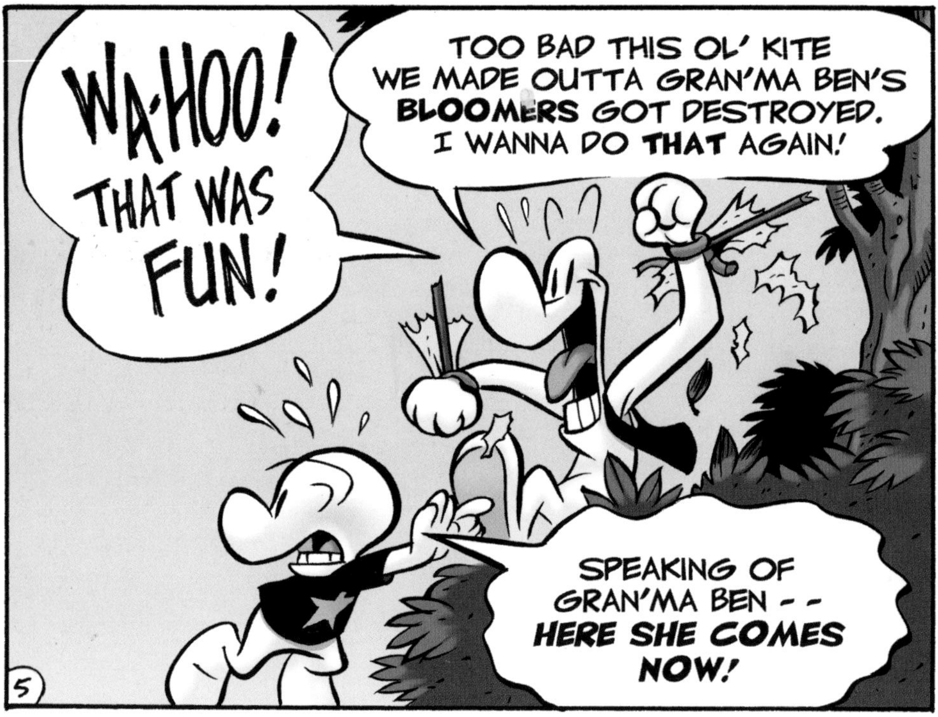
WA-HOO! THAT WAS FUN!
TOO BAD THIS OL' KITE WE MADE OUTTA GRAN'MA BEN'S BLOOMERS GOT DESTROYED. I WANNA DO THAT AGAIN!
SPEAKING OF GRAN'MA BEN - - HERE SHE COMES NOW!

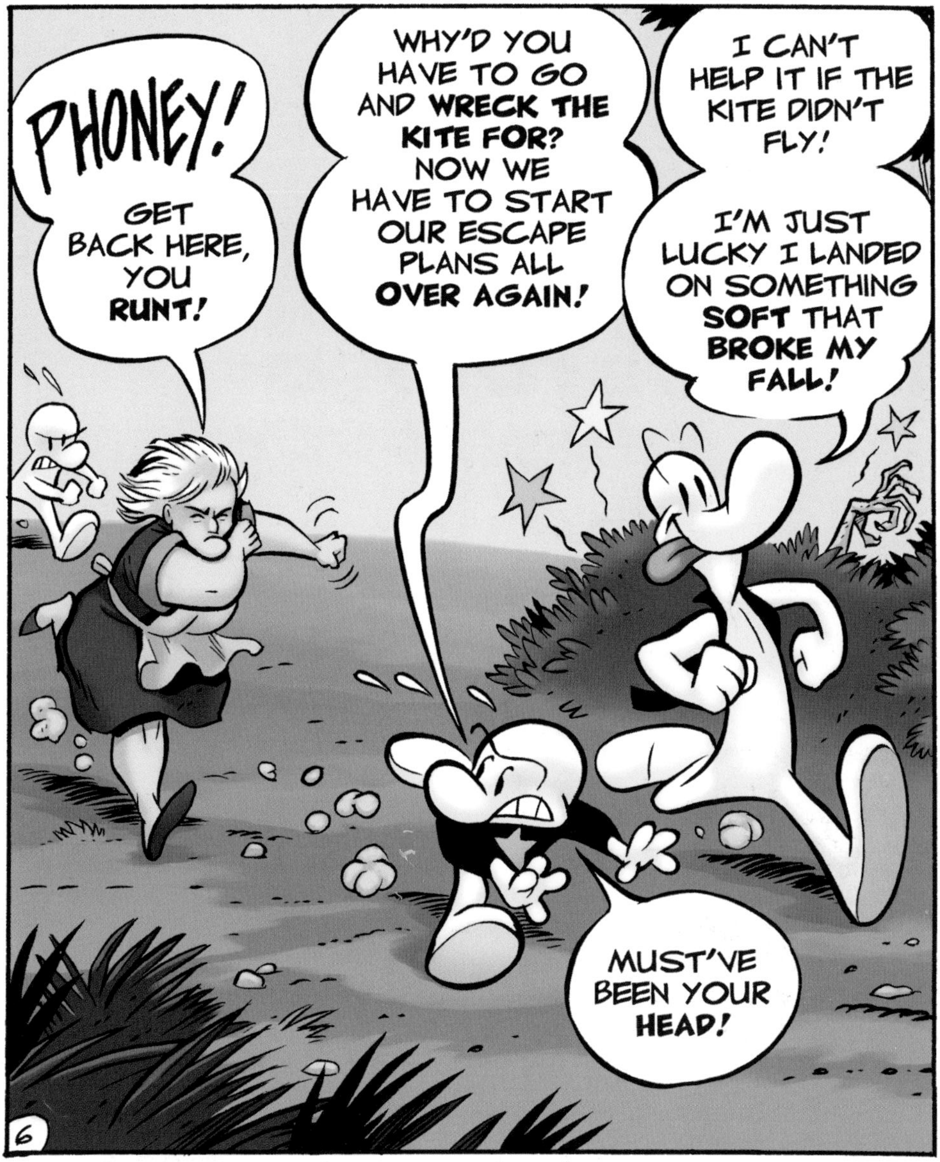
PHONEY!
GET BACK HERE, YOU RUNT!
WHY'D YOU HAVE TO GO AND WRECK THE KITE FOR? NOW WE HAVE TO START OUR ESCAPE PLANS ALL OVER AGAIN!
I CAN'T HELP IT IF THE KITE DIDN'T FLY!
I'M JUST LUCKY I LANDED ON SOMETHING SOFT THAT BROKE MY FALL!
MUST'VE BEEN YOUR HEAD!
6

The End

HISTORY OF THE VALLEY

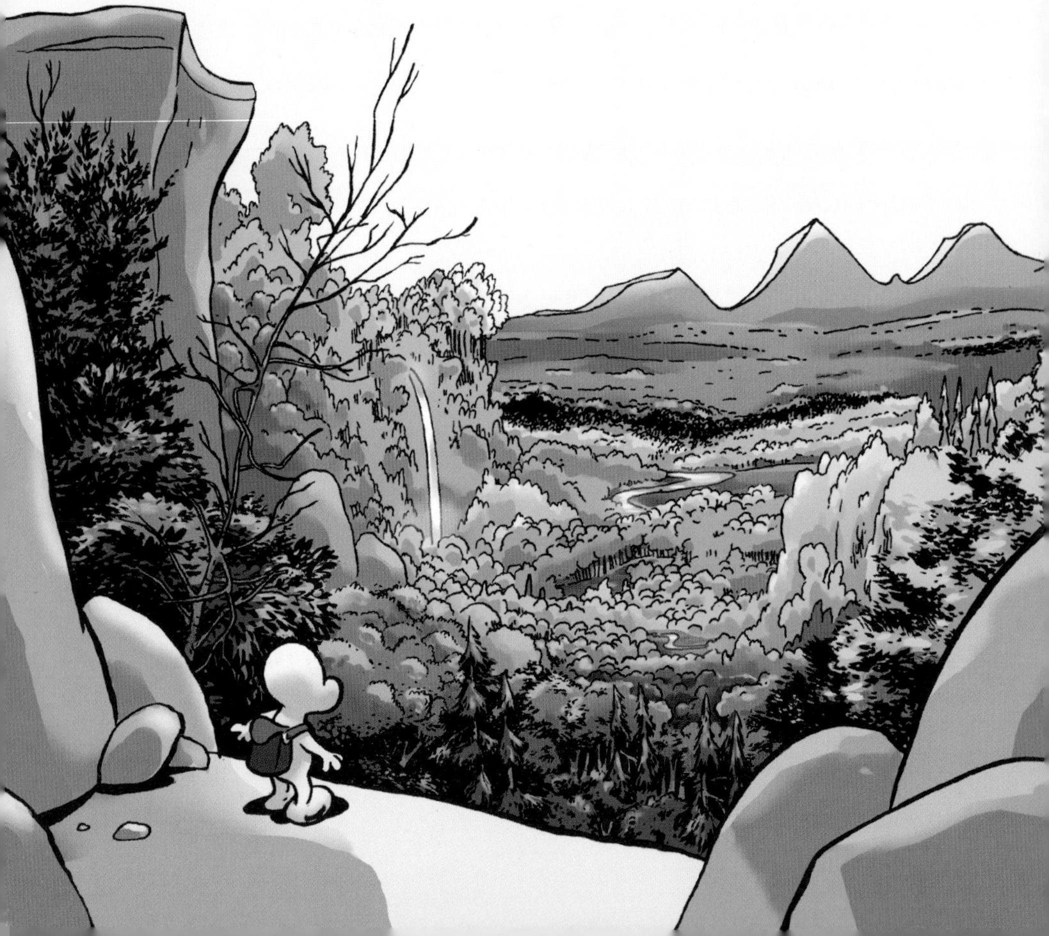

MIM VS. THE LORD OF THE LOCUSTS

IN THE BEGINNING, Dragons ruled the earth. The first Dragon was a queen named Mim. Mim was the largest, most beautiful, and wisest Dragon. She circled the world with her body and held her tail in her mouth. As long as the world was protected within her coil, the Dreaming flourished and all life thrived.

One day, a shapeless spirit known only as the Lord of the Locusts became jealous of Mim. In order to walk upon the world, the Locust needed to possess the flesh of a mortal being. For this he chose the greatest mortal of all: Mim, Queen of the Dragons.

As the Lord of the Locusts entered her mind, Mim went mad and let loose her tail. The world shook and the heavens thundered. The Dream became Nightmare.

The other Dragons were forced to battle their Queen to keep the world from being destroyed. A great war ensued, and many brave Dragons died as they fought back and forth, digging deep gullies, then crashing and pushing up mountains.

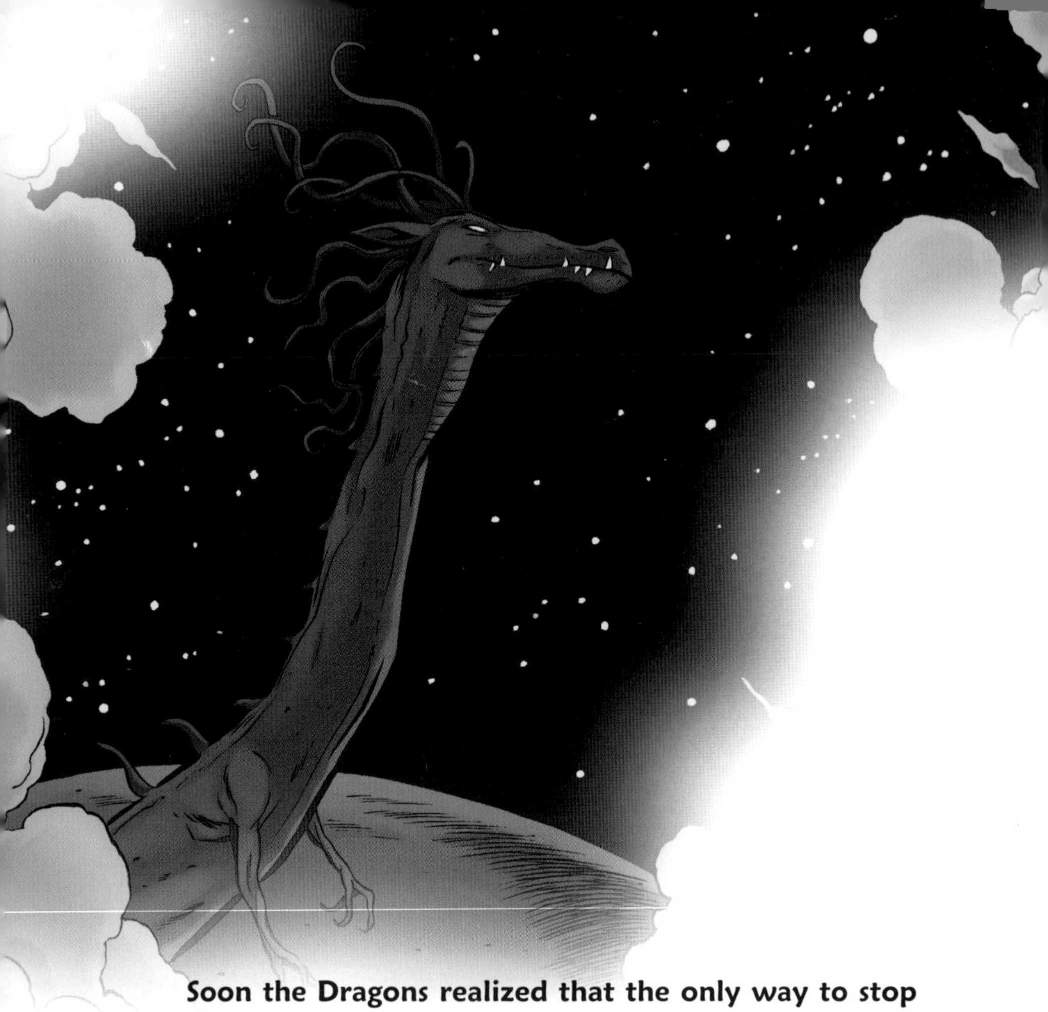

Soon the Dragons realized that the only way to stop the mad Queen and trap the true enemy within her was to turn Mim to stone. Together, they used their fire to turn their beloved Queen to rock, suspending her and the Locust forever in the roots of the Eastern Mountains.

The Dragons attempted to return the harmony of the Dreaming to the world, but the land would never again be perfect because the Lord of the Locusts lay below the surface.

The Dragons continued to Dream, practicing their arts in the hope that one day someone would be able to restore balance to the Dreaming and perhaps even destroy the Locust and free their Queen.

A SHORT HISTORY
OF DRAGONS, RAT CREATURES, AND
HUMANS IN THE VALLEY

AFTER THE FALL OF MIM, the Valley became a place of constant struggle as the Rat Creatures and the Dragons battled over the fertile lands between the Eastern and Western Mountains, often with the human population caught in the middle.

The Dragons decided to train humans in the arts of the Dreaming. The first human to receive the training was named Ven, who then became the first Queen of the new Human Kingdom.

In the early days, the alliance between humans and Dragons proved fruitful, and the Kingdom spread north, solidifying the humans' control of the Valley. The Rat Creatures were mostly relegated to the barren, stony hills of the Eastern Mountains, while the Dragons stayed in the west, using a series of interconnected underground caves and tunnels to travel from one end of the Valley to the other.

Eventually, the Dragons began to surface less and less often, withdrawing deeper and deeper into the earth,

leaving the fertile valley lands in the care of the humans. Some have speculated that the constant sight of their beloved Queen Mim frozen in stone was too much for them to bear.

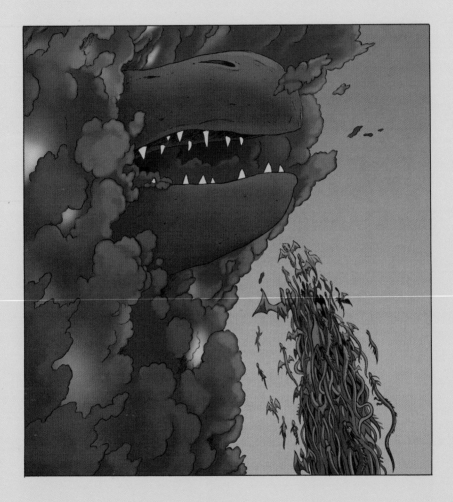

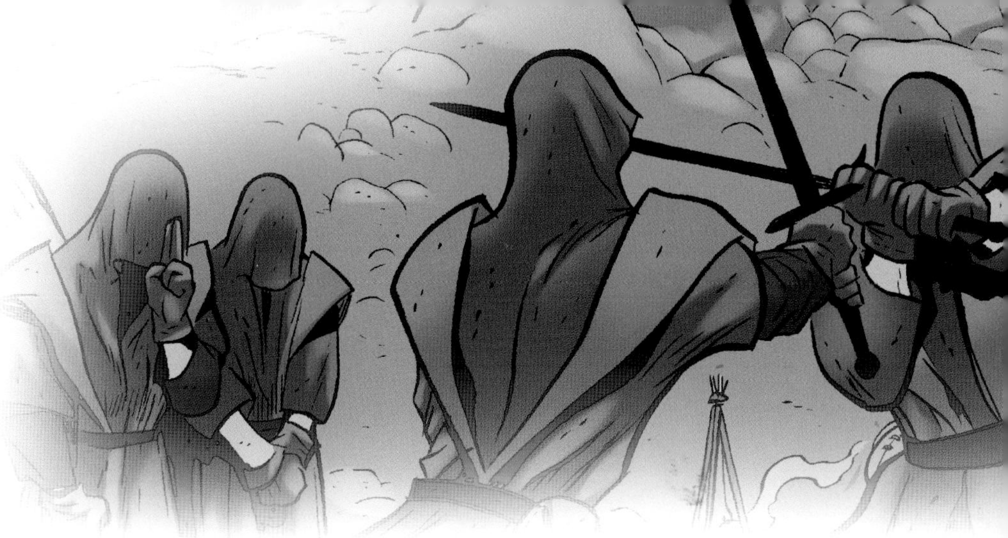

THE ORDER OF THE VENI YAN MONKS

THE MILITARY of the Kingdom was made up of a warrior/priest class called the Order of the Veni Yan – which translates roughly to "the Queen's Pupils" – who were charged with the protection of the Kingdom and were also the Keepers of the Wisdom of the Dreaming.

There were seven levels of Dream training. At least three were necessary to become a warrior, and five or higher were required to become a Dream Master. Dream Masters were rare, but rarer still was a Veni Yan Cari: an Awakened One able to be in the Waking World as well as in the Dreaming World, and capable of stretching his or her knowledge and senses over great distances.

Veni Yan monks were trained near the center of the Valley, deep in a beautiful gorge known as Old Man's Cave. Old Man's Cave is said to be the place where Ven received the wisdom of the Dreaming from the Dragons. It is also believed to be one of three sacred openings to the underground world of the Dragons, the others being Deren Gard in the north and Tanen Gard in the south.

RECENT EVENTS

AFTER GENERATIONS OF WAR with the Rat Creatures
(sometimes with the Dragons as allies, sometimes not),
the Old Kingdom has fallen into disarray. Most of the
Veni Yan order can now be found only in the southern
parts of the Valley, near the ancient city of Atheia. Very
few towns or villages in the far north have any lingering
ties with the Kingdom in the south. A Veni Yan who
still travels or lives in the north is generally treated by
the local denizens as a wandering holy man or a mystic.
Sometimes these holy men are treated with respect, but
more often, as people in the north forget the Dragons,
they are viewed with suspicion. A few monks still inhabit
their ancestral recesses in Old Man's Cave, but rarely
interact with people outside the order.

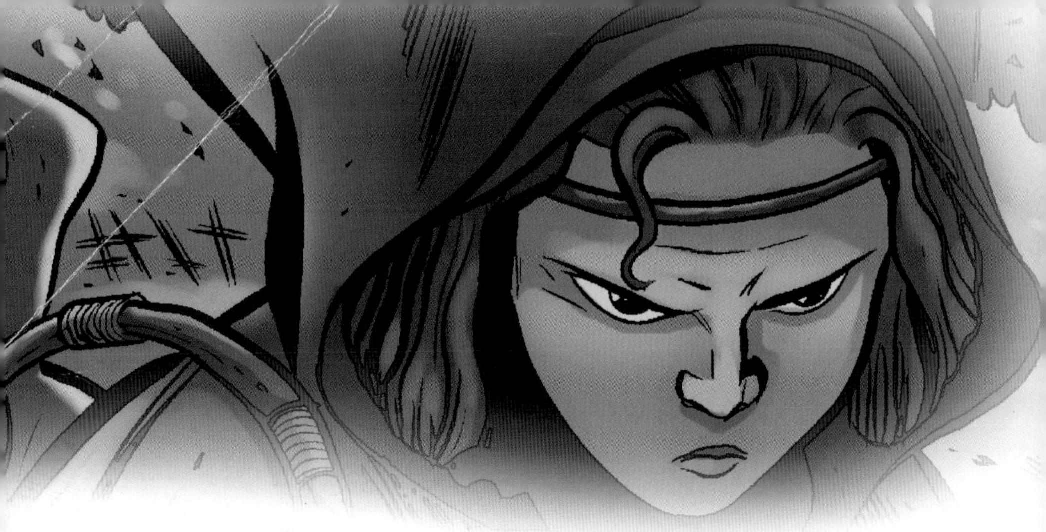

The wisdom of the Dragons is still taught in the cities of the south, but Dragons themselves are rarely seen by any humans. The only exceptions to this rule are the highest-level Dream Masters and members of the royal family.

Two sisters, Briar and Rose, are born to the Royal House of Harvestar. In keeping with tradition, both princesses are trained in the Dreaming arts, but to the royal family's dismay, it is soon discovered that the elder daughter's Dreaming eye is blind – a fact that will keep her from assuming the throne. The responsibility of heir apparent falls to the younger sibling, Rose. Unknown to Rose or anyone else, Briar is lying about her Dreaming eye, which is not blind at all. In fact, she is the most powerful Veni Yan Cari in a millennium. And she has been in constant contact with the imprisoned Lord of the Locusts since the moment she was born.

During Rose's Dream test, she unwittingly frees a rogue Dream Dragon, which sets in motion the Locust's plot to use Briar to free himself, and touches off the Great War between the Kingdom of Atheia and the Rat Creatures.

Later, Rose becomes Queen, and during the turbulent times that follow, she gives birth to a daughter named

Lunaria on the field of battle. While Queen Rose would long be known for her ability to wage war, as well as for the massive walls she built around Atheia, Lunaria – known to all who loved her as Moon – would be revered as a teacher, a builder of libraries, and a great patron of the arts. Moon takes a husband and gives birth to a beautiful baby girl. The Dragons claim they saw the birth of this child in their dreams – a sign that she might be a powerful Veni Yan Cari.

Briar, crippled but still alive after her earlier attempt to free the Locust, manages to keep her betrayal a secret from the rest of the royal family. She assumes the role of nursemaid to the infant princess, and at the same time forms an alliance with Kingdok, ruler of the Rat Creatures.

Briar concocts a plan to kidnap the young Veni Yan Cari, believing that a sacrifice by the Blood Moon will ensure the release of the Locust. Briar arranges to let Kingdok's army into the city.

FUN FACT: Did you know that Kingdok was designed with large hind legs that he walks on and small forelegs so that he looks similar to a *Tyrannosaurus rex*?

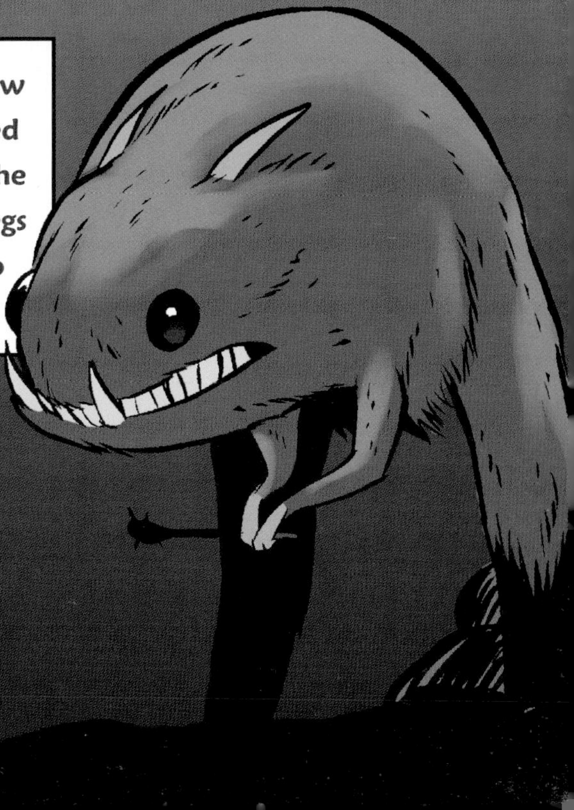

THE NIGHTS OF LIGHTNING

IN TWO NIGHTS of brutal attacks, the Rat Creatures sack the city of Atheia, but the royal family escapes via a secret tunnel provided to them by the Dragons. The tunnel leads the small party of travelers – Moon Harvestar, her husband, the young princess, Thorn, and Briar – high into the foothills of the Western Mountains. There they rendezvous with the queen mother, Rose, who is waiting to escort them to safety with the Dragons in Deren Gard.

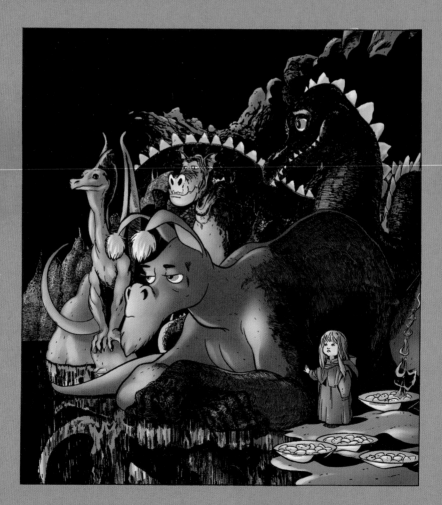

Briar gives a hidden signal and Kingdok attacks! Rose manages to get the baby to safety, personally handing her over to the Great Red Dragon, before rushing back to save the rest of her family. She finds a scene of carnage: Her daughter and son-in-law are dead, and Briar has been torn in two. The Rat Creatures are gone. Rose, alone and distraught, buries her family in the moonlight.

THE TREATY

THE WAR CONTINUES for three more years, and during this time Thorn is kept secretly with the Dragons. Rose, in desperation, finally agrees to a treaty. By its terms, the Rat Creatures will return to the Eastern Mountains and not set foot in the Valley without permission. The Dragons agree to stay underground or in the Western Mountains. And the humans can remain in the Valley as long as they promise to never rebuild the Kingdom.

At this time, Rose packs up her things and disappears from the lives and minds of everyone who knew her in the Old Kingdom. She quietly moves up to the far northern part of the Valley, near a very small village called Barrelhaven. There, where she is completely unknown to the local residents, she builds a small farm deep in the woods.

Rose changes her name from Harvestar to Ben and retrieves her granddaughter from the Dragons, who help suppress Thorn's memories of her time with them. Gran'ma Ben has one ally, the Captain of the Palace Guard, Lucius Down. He follows at a discreet distance and settles in Barrelhaven. Lucius buys the Tavern in the village and from there he keeps an eye on Rose and her granddaughter.

Occasionally, as Thorn gets older, the Red Dragon risks the treaty by coming aboveground and entering the Valley to visit Gran'ma Ben. Gently, he tries to coax the old woman to tell Thorn the truth about her past. The Dragon fears that the Rat Creatures are rebuilding their army and that Thorn needs to know the truth about who she is in order to reunite the Kingdom and hold the enemy at bay. But Gran'ma Ben won't hear of it. She has lost everyone dear to her except this little girl. She's done with war, with death – and she's done with Dragons. Year after year, the Red Dragon's entreaties are rebuffed.

As far as Gran'ma Ben is concerned, she and her granddaughter are going to live out their lives peacefully in that quiet little corner of the Valley, disappearing forever from the pages of history.

FUN FACT: Did you know that Thorn was the hardest character for Jeff to draw?

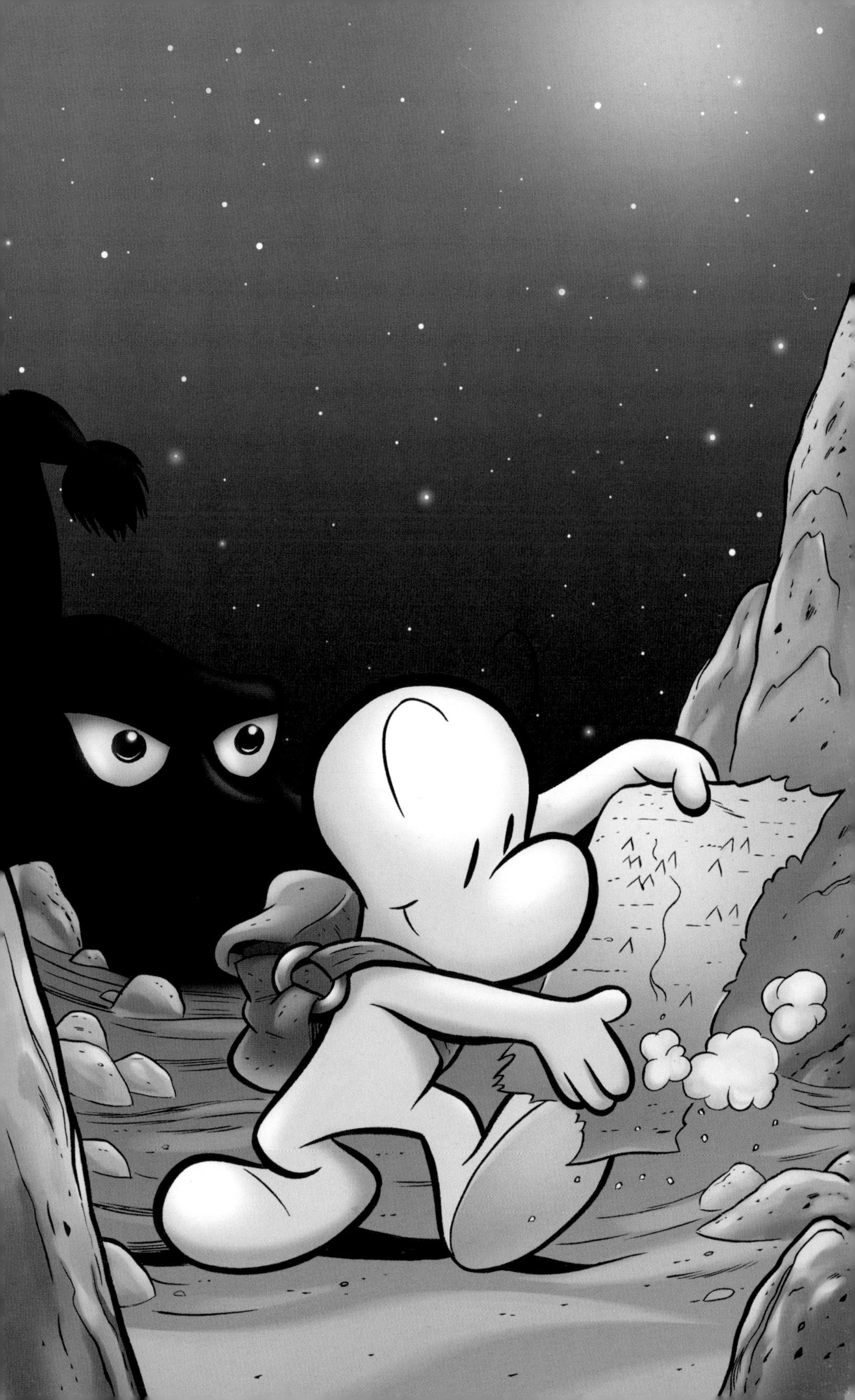

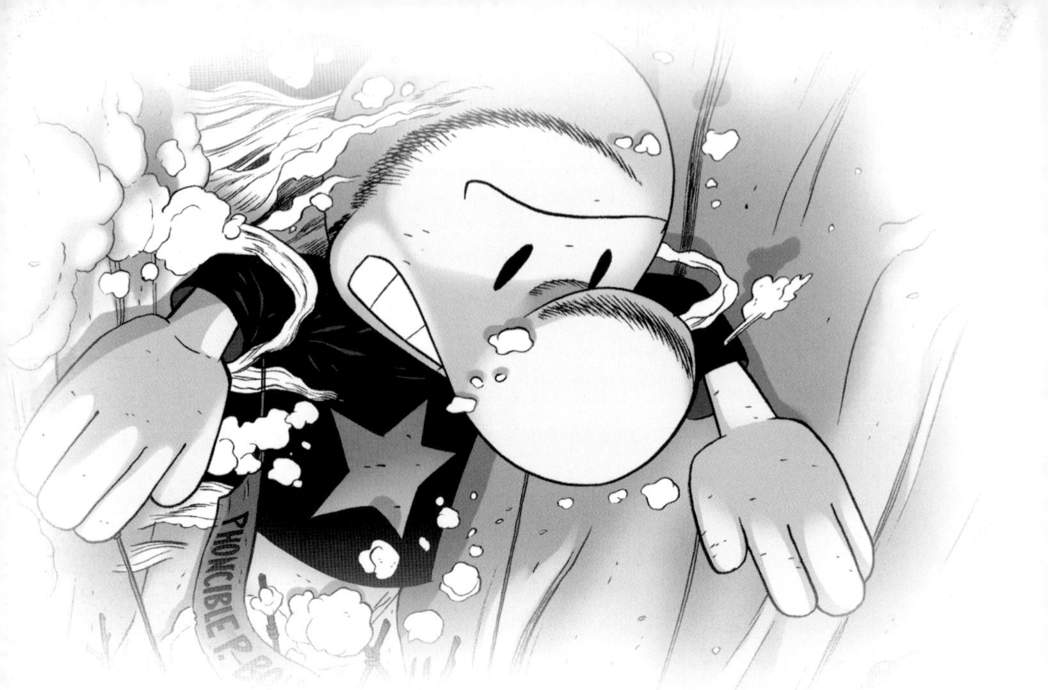
PHONCIBLE P.

ENTER THE BONES

FAR, FAR AWAY from the Valley, past the Western Mountains, beyond the vast desert wastelands, lies the bustling little burg of Boneville, where a celebration is taking place. One Phoncible P. Bone is throwing his hat into the ring for mayor. At his side are his two cousins, Fone Bone and Smiley Bone. Fone Bone and Smiley struggle to hold down a giant parade balloon shaped just like Phoncible (or "Phoney" for short). The balloon gets away, causes unbelievable chaos, and results in the three cousins being run out of town on a rail!

Meanwhile, the balloon floats free and drifts for days across the desert, over the mountains, across the Valley, and directly into the camp of Kingdok's new spiritual vizier, the Hooded One. The Hooded One is actually a resurrected Briar Harvestar. The Locust, unable to manipulate his freedom without her, used the Dreaming to reanimate the broken princess. After clawing her way out of her grave, Briar sought shelter with the ruler of the Rat Creatures, offering to share her knowledge of the Dreaming with him.

The arrival of the Phoney Bone–shaped balloon alarms the Hooded One, for she remembers an old Dragon prophecy that claimed that "the one who bears the star will either free the Locust or kill it." In the middle of the balloon-Phoney's shirt (as well as on the real Phoney) is a giant gold star.

Fearing that the balloon is a warning of an invasion of some sort, the Hooded One stretches out her mind and senses the presence of the Bones in the desert beyond the Western Mountains. She sends her swarm of locusts out to investigate. . . .

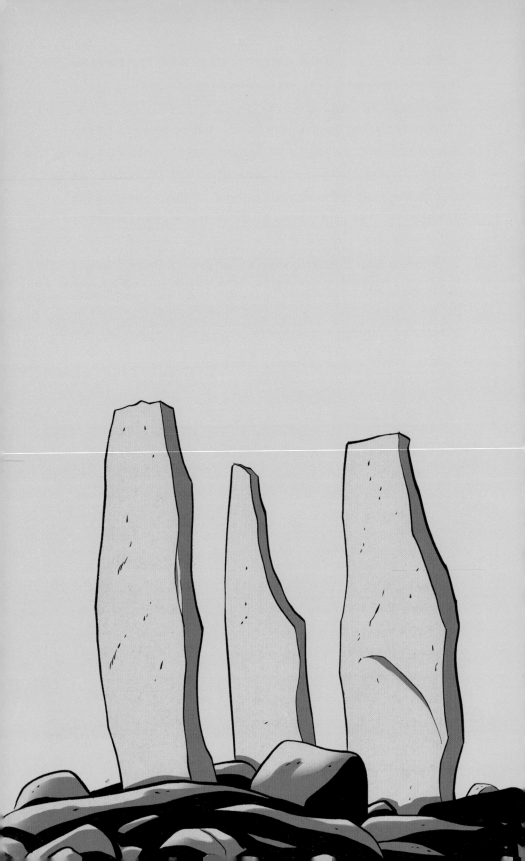

BOOK ONE:
OUT FROM BONEVILLE

THE BONE COUSINS are lost in the middle of a vast, uncharted desert. Smiley spots a crudely drawn map, but before they can find their way, the Bones are driven off in different directions by a swarm of locusts.

After a run-in with two stupid Rat Creatures and the Red Dragon, Fone Bone comes to the Valley, where he meets Ted the Bug. He spends the winter babysitting the Possum Kids, and when they're nearly captured by the two stupid Rat Creatures, the Red Dragon shows up in the nick of time!

Fone Bone meets Thorn, and before long, he's fallen head over heels. Fone Bone and Phoney reunite at Gran'ma Ben's farm, and after some convincing, she agrees to let them stay.

The Hooded One instructs her Rat Creature army to find Phoney, destroy Gran'ma Ben's farmhouse, and kill Fone Bone. When they attack, the Red Dragon saves the day again. And when Phoney goes to the Barrelhaven Tavern, he discovers that Smiley is the bartender. Together, they hatch a plan to fix the Great Cow Race at the Spring Fair.

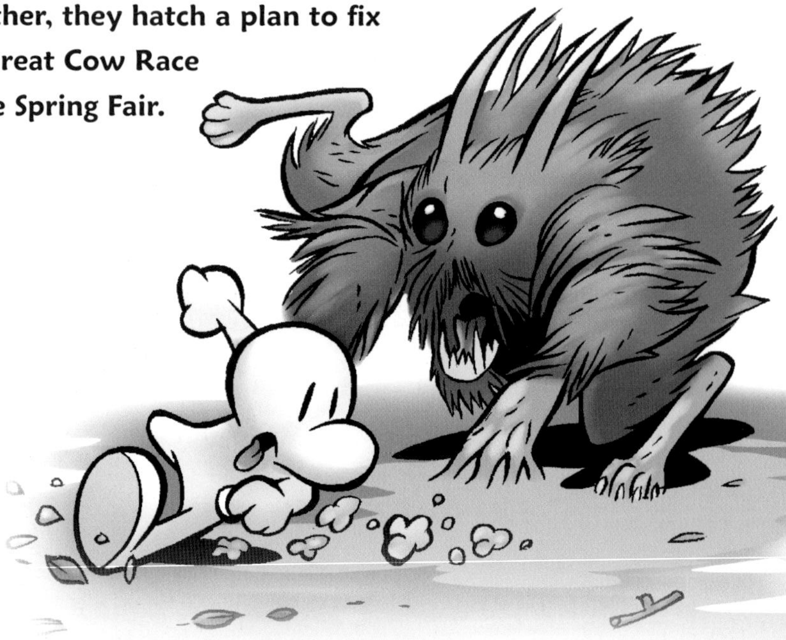

BOOK TWO: THE GREAT COW RACE

THE SPRING FAIR has arrived! Phoney and Smiley take bets on the Great Cow Race after spreading rumors that Gran'ma Ben isn't as fast as she used to be. But Lucius places a large bet on Gran'ma Ben, anyway, and now the Mystery Cow has to win! Phoney tries to help by climbing into the costume with Smiley.

And the race is on! Phoney and Smiley veer off the path into a group of sleeping Rat Creatures. Meanwhile, Fone Bone is being chased by the two stupid Rat

Creatures. Fone Bone and the Mystery Cow lead the Rat Creatures right into the path of Gran'ma Ben and the racing cows, which causes a huge pileup. Villagers who lost money on the race chase the Bones, Gran'ma Ben, Thorn, and Lucius out of town, and Phoney gets what he deserves.

Back at the farmhouse, Gran'ma Ben thinks the Rat Creatures attacked the farm because they were looking for the Bones, and decides to delay telling Thorn about her heritage.

FUN FACT: Did you know that the Possum Kids are Jeff Smith's homage to Walt Kelly's famous possum, Pogo?

BOOK THREE:
EYES OF THE STORM

AFTER AN ENCOUNTER with the Rat Creatures and the Red Dragon, Gran'ma Ben finally tells Thorn and the Bones more about the Great War and Thorn's royal heritage. Thorn is actually the crown princess of Atheia and has a lot of enemies!

Lucius and Phoney make a bet on which of them can attract the most customers at the Tavern. Phoney's schemes have little effect, and Lucius takes an early lead. But when Smiley mentions their encounters with the Red Dragon, everyone is suddenly interested, and Phoney doesn't hesitate to introduce himself as the "Dragonslayer."

A Veni Yan warrior brings news of Rat Creatures headed toward Barrelhaven. Ted the Bug carries this news to Gran'ma Ben, who grabs a sword and shield from a hidden trunk and flees the farm with Fone Bone and Thorn.

BOOK FOUR:
THE DRAGONSLAYER

DURING A FIGHT with the Rat Creatures and Kingdok, Thorn cuts off Kingdok's right arm and Fone Bone takes his war club. Thorn doesn't trust Gran'ma Ben, and Thorn and Fone Bone head to the Barrelhaven Tavern without her.

There's a new boss in Barrelhaven! Lucius doesn't like how Phoney the "Dragonslayer" has stirred up the townspeople's fear of the Dragons, but the townspeople are on Phoney's side.

Fone Bone finds a Rat Creature cub in the village. When he shows it to Smiley, a friendship is born. Soon, Fone Bone and Smiley sneak out of the village, hoping to return the cub to his horde.

Wendell is tired of hiding from the Dragons and wants Phoney to earn his keep, so they and the townsfolk head out on a Dragonslaying quest. They set up traps at Dragon's Stair and almost immediately catch the Red Dragon! (He allowed himself to be captured, of course.)

The townspeople want to kill the Red Dragon, but Phoney isn't sure. Thorn appears and tells them to set the Dragon free, but suddenly several Rat Creatures sneak up and see their greatest enemy tied up. Veni Yan warriors arrive and attack the Rat Creatures, Thorn frees the Red

Dragon, and reality sets in for the villagers: They're in the middle of a war.

BOOK FIVE:
ROCK JAW: MASTER OF
THE EASTERN BORDER

AFTER ANOTHER CLOSE SCRAPE with the two stupid Rat Creatures, Fone Bone, Smiley, and the cub – now named Bartleby – meet Rock Jaw. The Possum Kids and Roderick follow Fone Bone and Smiley through the forest, and they lead the Rat Creatures on a chase right to Rock Jaw!

The Bones, the Possum Kids, and a group of orphaned animals escape through a secret passage in the mountains that opens onto an ancient stone temple. Kingdok appears and calls the two stupid Rat Creatures traitors. He knocks them all off a cliff onto a ledge. The group scrambles to escape, and when a locust swarm tries to grab Fone Bone, the Dragon necklace scares it away.

The group heads into the forest, but Rock Jaw finds them and herds them back up the mountain. They once again meet Kingdok, who scares Rock Jaw away, and the two stupid Rat Creatures offer the Bones to Kingdok. The orphans attack the two stupid Rat Creatures, and the Bones escape.

While Rock Jaw attacks Kingdok, the Bones and the orphans scatter into the woods. Bartleby goes with the two stupid Rat Creatures, who carry Kingdok away.

FUN FACT: Did you know that Bartleby was named by a fan for the title character in the short story "Bartleby the Scrivener" by Herman Melville?

BOOK SIX:
OLD MAN'S CAVE

THE RAT CREATURES have destroyed much of Barrel-haven and are securing their positions throughout the Valley. A group of them surround Fone Bone and Smiley in the forest. Thorn steps in and tosses Kingdok's war club to Fone Bone, and the Rat Creatures run away.

Briar visits Lucius in her human form in order to distract him from setting up defenses at Old Man's Cave so the Rat Creatures can sneak in and attack.

Thorn, Fone Bone, and Smiley return to the farm-house, where Thorn prepares for battle. Rock Jaw, who has made a deal with the Hooded One, shows up, sniffing around for Thorn and the Bones.

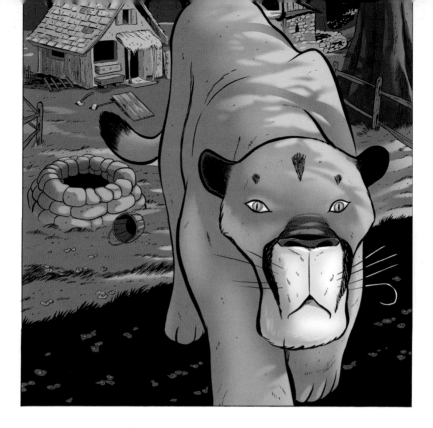

The Rat Creatures slaughter many townspeople and Veni Yan warriors, and the Dragons have retired underground, unwilling to fight despite Gran'ma Ben's pleas.

Gran'ma Ben finds Phoney, who has run away, on a mountain trail. Rock Jaw attacks them, and Phoney escapes and runs smack into Fone Bone, Thorn, and Smiley. There's a fight, and Rock Jaw catches Phoney and Thorn.

Fone Bone, Smiley, and Gran'ma Ben follow Rock Jaw to the temple ruins, where Phoney is tied to a ritual altar. Phoney won't join the Hooded One in the ritual, so she threatens to sacrifice him instead. A massive earthquake strikes before the ritual can be completed, and the Bones, Gran'ma Ben, and Thorn rush to escape the crumbling ruins.

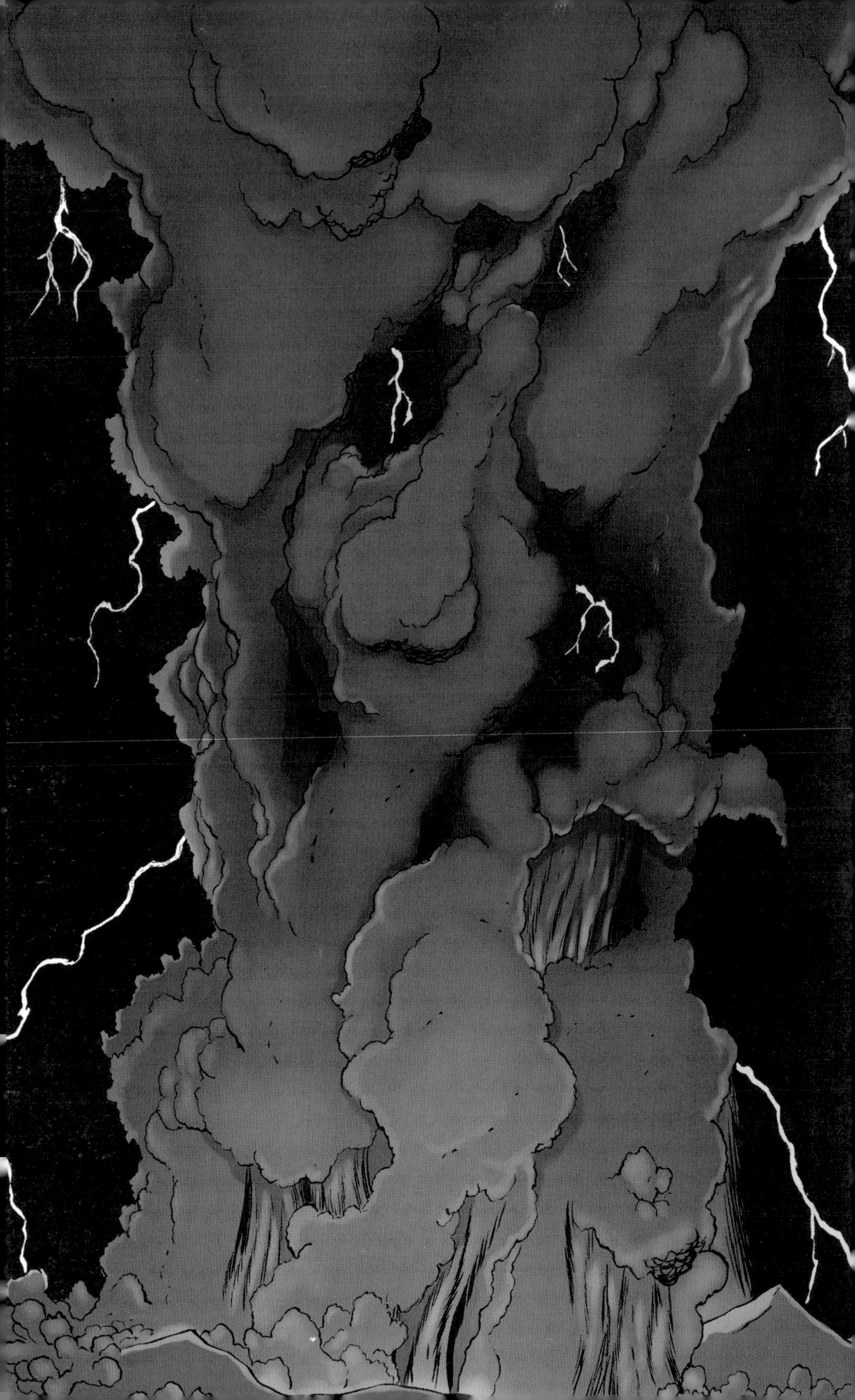

BOOK SEVEN:
GHOST CIRCLES

GRAN'MA BEN AND THE BONES follow Thorn through the ghost circles Briar has unleashed across the Valley. Thorn can tell where they are and can even travel in and out of them!

Rat Creatures – including Bartleby – attack, and Briar sets her sights on Fone Bone. But here come Smiley and Bartleby to the rescue! They all continue south toward Atheia, and when Fone Bone and Thorn step inside a ghost circle to look for food, a voice urges Thorn to seek the "Crown of Horns."

Rat Creatures attack **Old Man's Cave**, and **Lucius** convinces the Veni Yan to go to Atheia for any hope of survival.

FUN FACT: Did you know that the eruption of Mount St. Helens in Washington State in 1980 inspired the scene of an ash-covered Valley and locusts bursting out of a mountain?

BOOK EIGHT: TREASURE HUNTERS

ONCE GRAN'MA BEN, the Bones, and Thorn get inside the gates of Atheia, they meet with Gran'ma Ben's former teacher, a Dream Master. Thorn falls into a trance when Briar tries to contact her, and the teacher keeps Thorn awake with herbal tea once she's brought back to her senses.

Phoney and Fone Bone chase off a giant bee in the central marketplace, and the Atheians offer Phoney gold as a reward – and promise him more if he comes back every day to do it again. Now Phoney's sure there's treasure to be found!

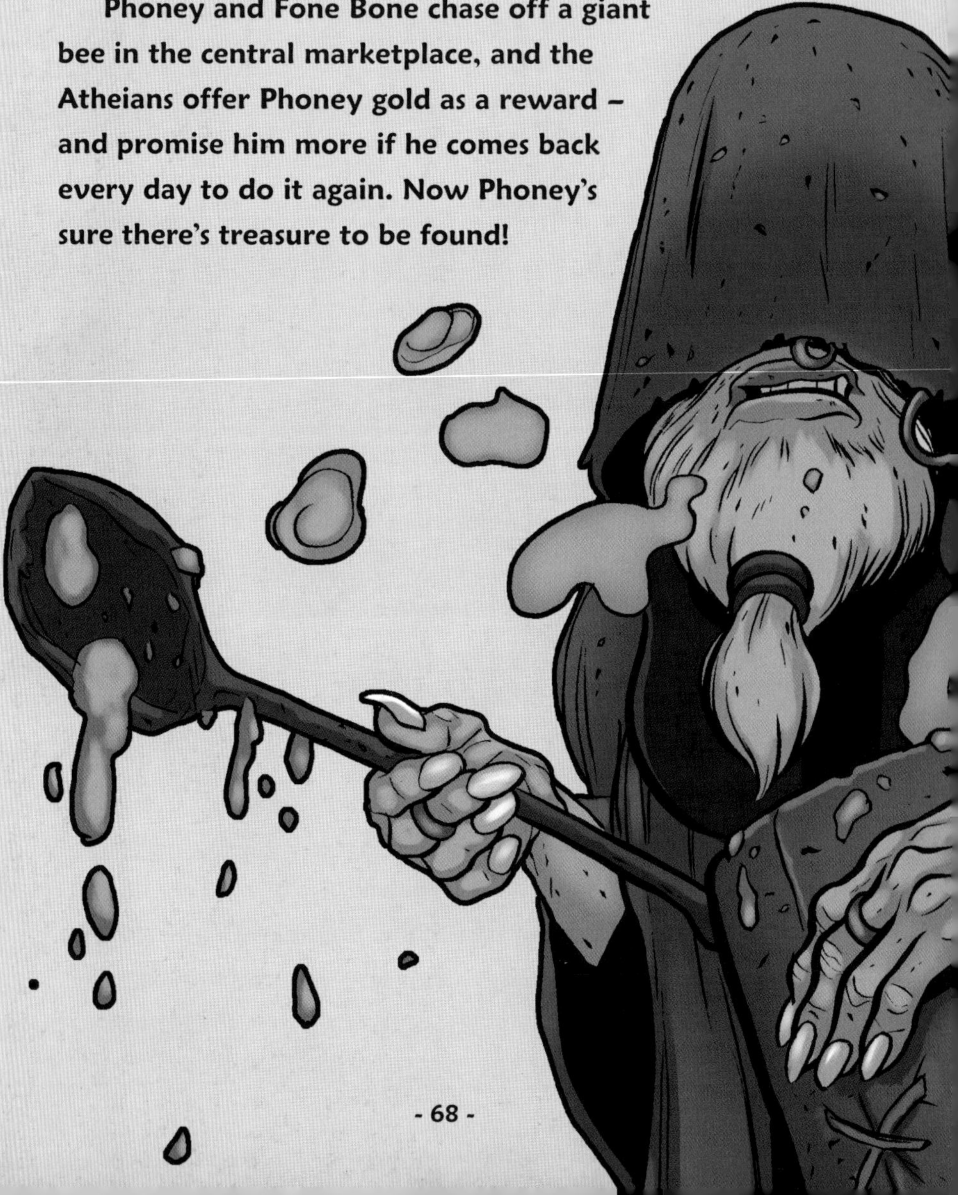

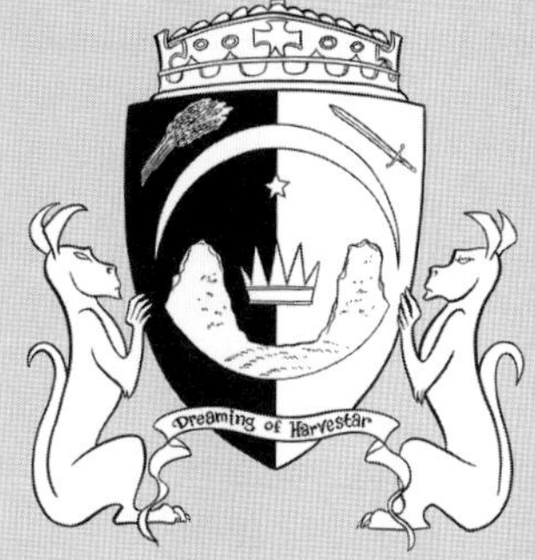
Dreaming of Harvestar

FUN FACT: Did you know that the Harvestar clan motto is "Dreaming of Harvestar"?

Fone Bone rushes into a meeting that Gran'ma Ben, Thorn, and Phoney are having with the Atheian resistance to report that Lord Tarsil, who has ordered them captured, knows they're in the city. The teacher doesn't trust Thorn, an untrained Veni Yan Cari, to lead them, until Thorn reveals the message about the Crown of Horns. But he's afraid that if Thorn touches the Crown of Horns, all of existence will end.

Phoney thinks the city's treasure is hidden in the well in the marketplace, but when he and Smiley go there, the Vedu capture them.

Thorn and Fone Bone are arrested while trying to protect Taneal, who has been caught building a Dragon shrine. Meanwhile, the alarm sounds as the Pawan army and Rat Creatures attack the royal city.

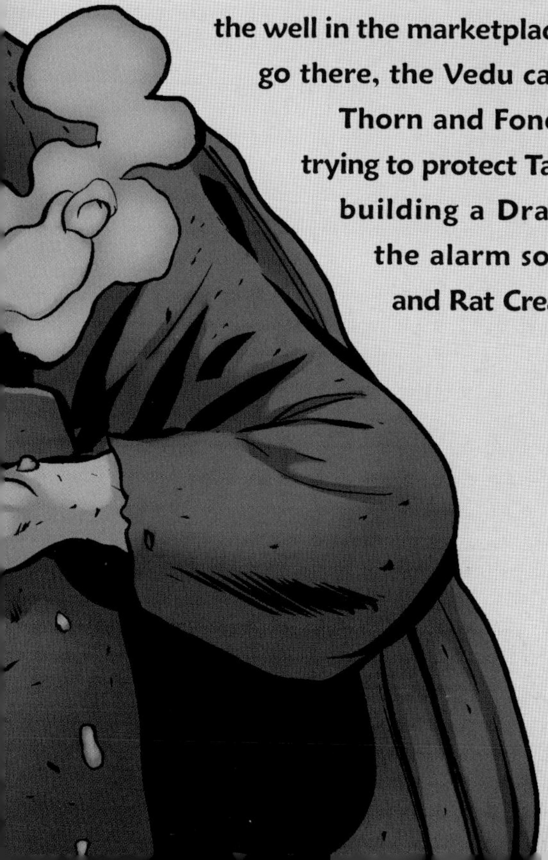

BOOK NINE:
CROWN OF HORNS

THORN AND FONE BONE have been badly beaten and thrown into an Atheian dungeon, and Smiley and Phoney are in the cell next to them.

Briar offers Lord Tarsil a chance to surrender. He refuses, and Briar kills him before ordering her army to attack the city.

The Vedu join the Veni Yan warriors and listen to Gran'ma Ben's orders. But the enemy overwhelms Gran'ma Ben, and Mermie creates a vision to scare their attackers away. Thorn and the Bones escape the dungeon and join the battle.

There is a huge explosion as the Lord of the Locusts frees both himself and Mim. A swarm of locusts heads toward Atheia, and Mim is in the center of it!

Phoney and Smiley have finally found the treasure. Phoney tells Thorn he thinks the Crown of Horns is in Tanen Gard, and Thorn immediately goes to look for it. She disappears into a ghost circle when the Rat Creatures chase her, and when she comes out of it she collides with Fone Bone and

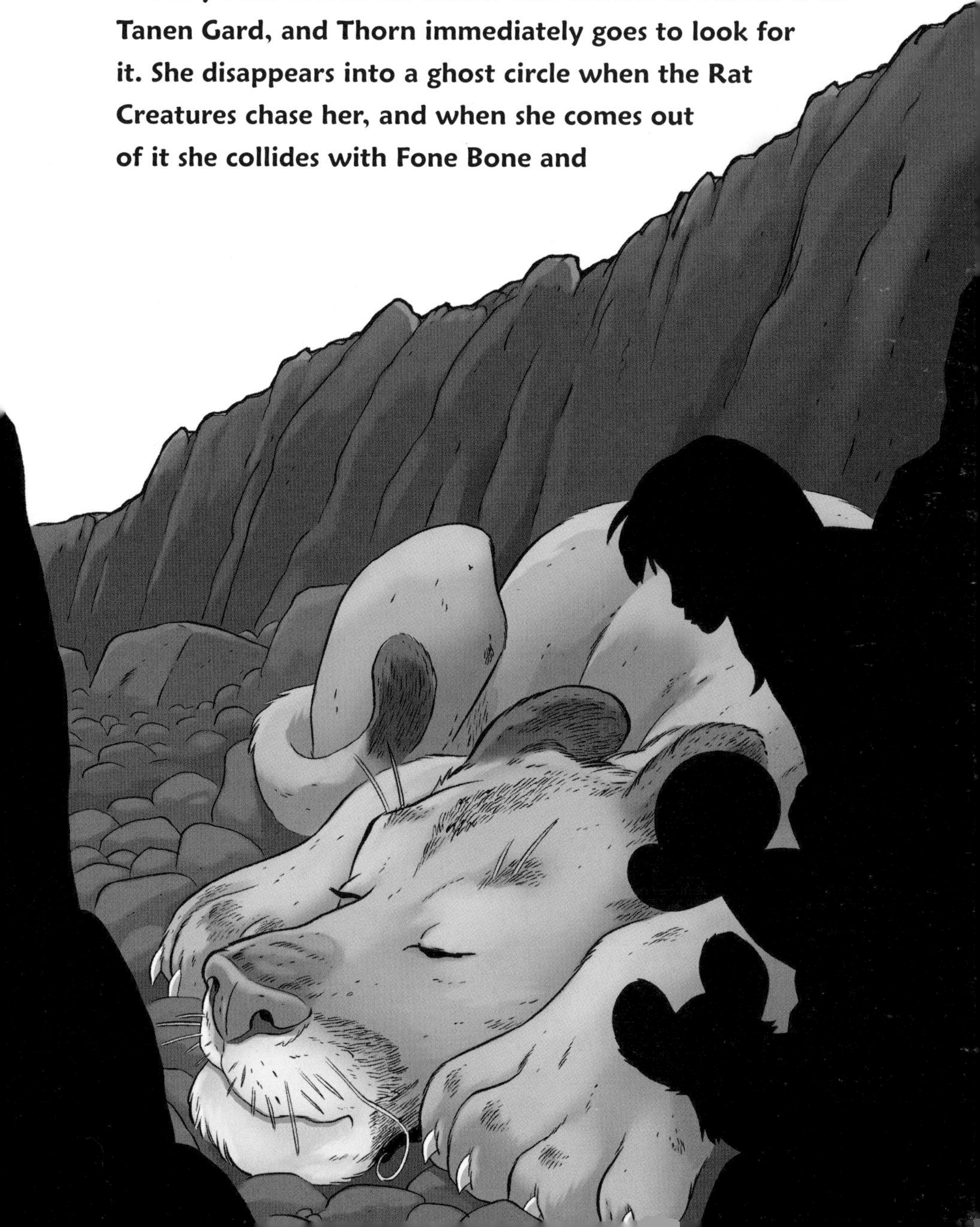

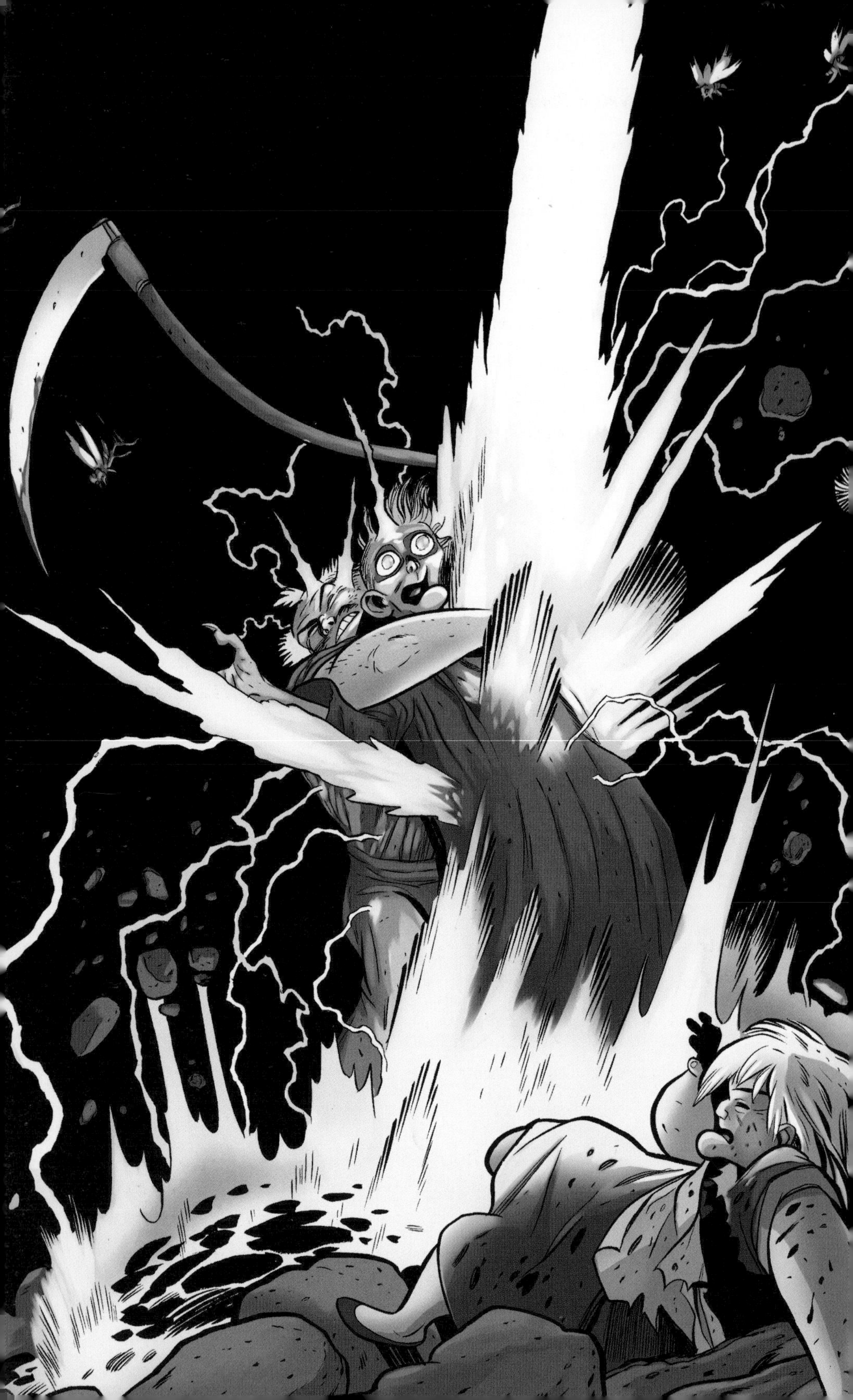

Bartleby, who have followed her. They are separated again while making their escape from the enemy army.

Thorn has reached the Crown of Horns, but Kingdok is guarding it. As she tries to get past him, Kingdok bites her in the leg, and she stabs him through the eye. Thorn is trapped in the dead Kingdok's clenched teeth and can't quite touch the Crown of Horns.

Fone Bone reaches Thorn and, in desperation, grabs her hand and touches the Crown of Horns. A huge bolt of lightning shoots from it and strikes Briar and Lucius on Sinner's Rock. The Veni Yan declare victory, but the Dragons have awakened and they're very, very angry!

As the Red Dragon helps Thorn and Fone Bone escape from Tanen Gard, the Rat Creatures and the Pawan army prepare another attack. The Red Dragon easily defeats them, and then the other Dragons drive Mim back underground. Phoney and Smiley arrive with reinforcements, but by then the battle is finally over.

Later, Thorn is crowned Queen of Atheia and Lucius is buried in a quiet ceremony near the Barrelhaven Tavern. Back at Gran'ma Ben's farmhouse, Phoney is anxious to finally get back to Boneville, and Fone Bone admits that he's already decided to go back, too. And so has Bartleby! They pack up the hay cart and make their way through the forest to the edge of the desert . . . with Boneville just beyond the horizon.

FUN FACT: Did you know that Smiley Bone is something of a tribute to the character Wimpy from the original *Popeye* cartoons, just as Gran'ma Ben is in part a tribute to Popeye himself?

A CONVERSATION WITH JEFF SMITH

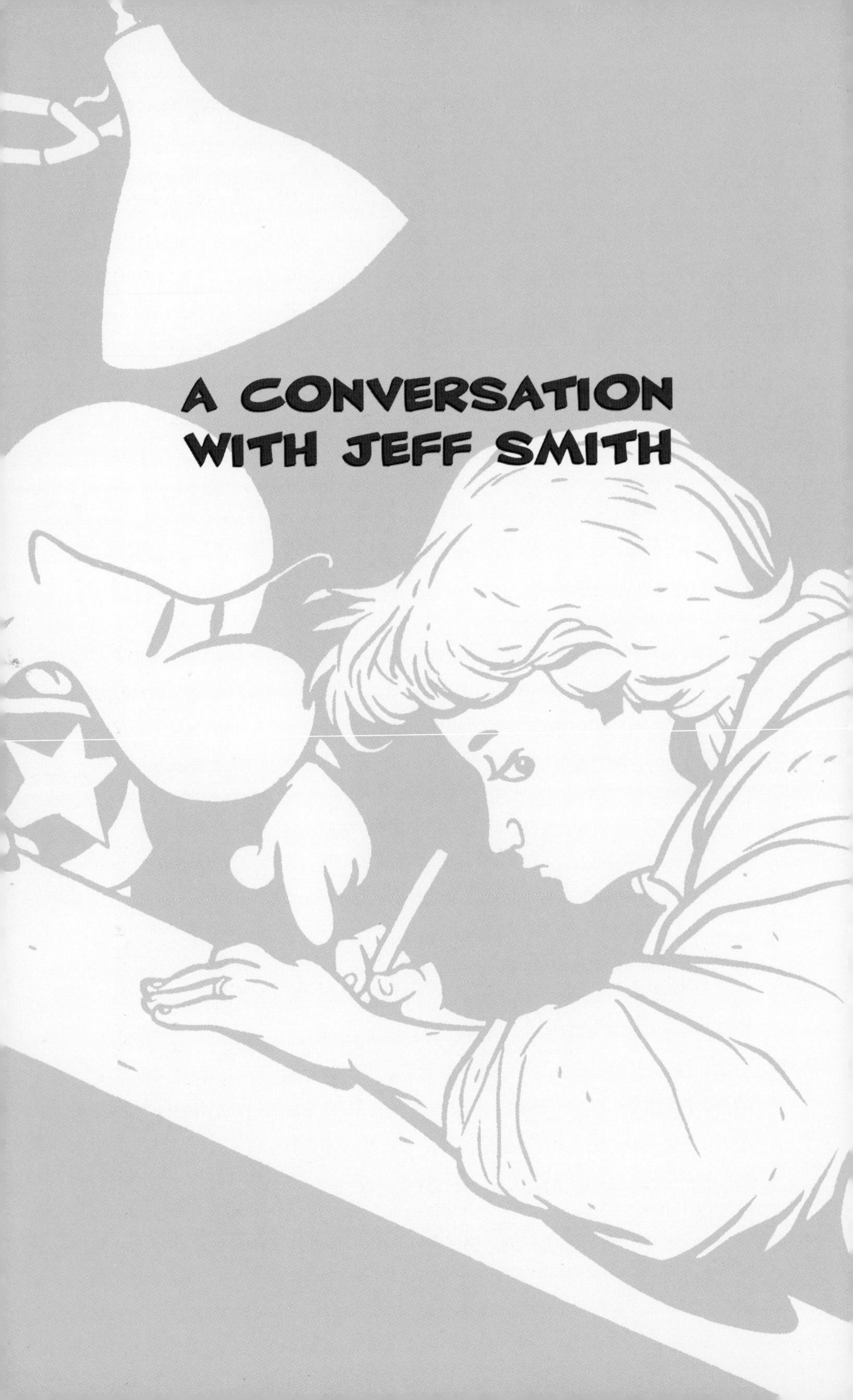

What were you able to take from growing up in Ohio and later add into *BONE*?

A lot of people think that Ohio is flat farmland, but where I grew up in south central Ohio, it's actually very rolling country. There are cliffs, waterfalls, caves, trees – just like in the Valley. It makes it all kind of magical. As a kid, I would imagine stories taking place in all those places. The settings in *BONE* are all based on where I grew up. For example, Old Man's Cave is based on a real cave in Hocking Hills State Park, near Columbus. I always wanted to infuse my comics work with how special nature is.

On the left is a photo of the real-life Old Man's Cave, and on the right side this image transitions into Jeff's illustration.

Did you receive encouragement for your drawing when you were younger?

My family encouraged me a lot – especially my grand-mothers. My maternal grandmother had an artistic side, and she was always giving me crayons to draw with. And my other grandmother was really into stories and read Grimm's fairy tales to me – not the sanitized versions, but the really scary ones. Those two influences eventually came together in *BONE*.

I had good teachers and a good principal in grammar school. My teachers there encouraged me a lot. Later on in high school and college, not so much. I was run out of a couple universities because I wanted to be a cartoonist, and they didn't have very much respect for cartoons and comics as art forms – fine art and commercial art were the only options. When I asked one of my professors how I could tailor my program toward comics, he basically told me I needed to either forget them or get out.

When did you know you wanted to draw comics for a living?

Well, there are two ways of describing the desire of wanting to do something. I loved cartoons so much as a kid that I knew I'd like to do that. There's something about the panels in comics – they're like little windows into your imagination that you could almost fall into. It was a powerful thing to me.

As a grown-up, I have no idea when I realized I wanted to do comics for a living. After I got out of college, I started drawing little comics that people I knew actually laughed at ("Stupid, Stupid Rat Creatures," for instance). I couldn't stop myself once I got started.

How did the original _BONE_ comic series get started?

Originally I tried to do _BONE_ as a comic strip and couldn't sell it. The King and Tribune [newspaper syndicates] kind of liked it, but wanted to make too many changes – like getting rid of the girl and the Dragon, and doing a joke a day, and having the characters talk in thought balloons.

I thought the editors were nuts. I tried to trick them into liking it, but still nobody liked it.

Then I found comic book stores with a very healthy independent scene and did a bunch of research about how to get into the [comic distribution] catalogs. There wasn't a lot of competition then because I was one of the first independents. *Teenage Mutant Ninja Turtles* had been self-published a few years earlier, and the question a lot of retailers were asking was, "What's the next *Teenage Mutant Ninja Turtles*?" And I thought maybe it could be *BONE*.

How much of *BONE*'s story did you have planned out before you actually started working on it, and how closely did you stick to that plan?

I had a goal in mind, but I didn't necessarily have a detailed plan on how to get there. I wrote the ending for the story in 1989, and that last page was the exact same one that I drew in 2004 for the final issue of the *BONE* series, with the Bone cousins riding away downhill. So I had the entire story arc planned out, very broadly. Knowing what it was I was aiming for, I was able to work backwards.

I deliberately eased my way into the story. I started with just the Bones, a fairly familiar set of characters – Fone Bone, Phoney, and Smiley are Mickey, Donald, and Goofy; they're Bugs Bunny, Daffy Duck, and Porky Pig – and with simple Disney-type adventures, and just proceeded to let the characters fall into the adventure, just the way you fall into adventures in real life.

Because I had the backstory all worked out before I started, I was constantly vigilant about only adding story points that would either add to a character's development or move the story along. Also, an important part of storytelling, especially in comics, is knowing when to leave blank spaces. Going in, I knew where all the villages and landmarks were in the Valley, and I pretty much knew the whole history of Atheia, but I thought it was more interesting to let all that unfold gradually instead of just all being dumped on the reader up front. I wanted to leave room for the characters and the settings to develop, so I didn't finalize a lot of the details until the end.

FUN FACT: Did you know that Jeff Smith decided to never show Boneville because everyone he got feedback from had an entirely different idea of what it might look like?

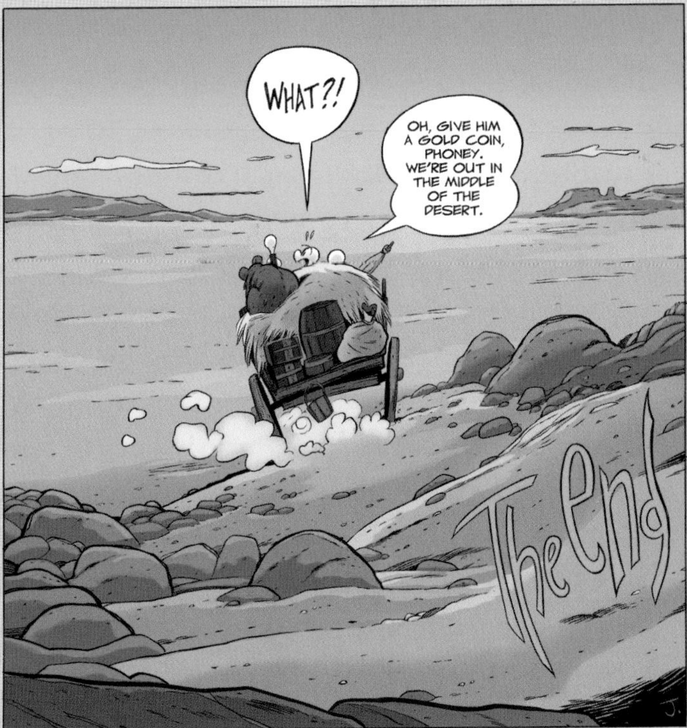
WHAT?!
OH, GIVE HIM A GOLD COIN, PHONEY. WE'RE OUT IN THE MIDDLE OF THE DESERT.
The End
J.

What was your process of writing and drawing BONE like?

I write and draw simultaneously to get an organic mix of the pictures and words at the same time. First I create thumbnail sketches showing layouts of the pages and tack them to a wall in the order they'll appear in the story, to get a clear picture of what the story will look like.

For each page, after it's been laid out, I enlarge it and reproduce it onto the actual artboard using non-reproducible blue pencil. Then I compose the final black-and-white line work over that.

It takes me about a year to do a 120-page graphic novel – about two days per page. But in between the time spent actually drawing, I may spend days on my couch just thinking about the story and how to do it.

I pictured everything in the world of BONE when I was creating the pages. I playacted. Once I got my imagination going, it could get intense – like one scene where Fone Bone is being chased by Rat Creatures up over rock outcroppings and cliffs and waterfalls. I was with him the whole time. I was gritting my teeth, thinking what it's like being chased by monsters. I would get exhausted after days of thinking about that stuff.

Do you have a favorite *BONE* character, or one that you identify most with?

Phoney was the most fun to write, but as far as identifying with him . . . Well, I've certainly met people like Phoney Bone, but I rarely maintain relationships with them. In fact, I usually try to put as much distance between them and myself as possible! Phoney does have a redeeming quality, however, and that's his loyalty. And loyalty is a really integral part of the story – maybe even what it's all about.

And then there's Rock Jaw. The ambivalence he shows about choosing one side or the other pretty much sums up the philosophical heart of *BONE*: It's up to you to decide who your loyalties are with, and it's up to you to make the most out of your life.

Do you have any advice for kids aspiring to be comic book artists?

Draw. I'm gratified that people I knew when I was a kid are now contacting me to tell me their kids are reading *BONE*. Some of them, in fact, have asked me if I could tell their children that cartooning is great – but just don't draw in class. But . . . I wouldn't dare tell the kids not to draw in class! Draw, draw, draw. As much as you can, as much as you want. And learn everything you can about comics and graphic novels. Read the ones you like, including everything your favorite creators have done.

HOW BONE WAS COLORED

STEVE HAMAKER, pictured above, begins by scanning Jeff's original black-and-white art into the computer at a very high resolution. He uses a large scanner that can accommodate the size of Jeff's 14" x 17" artboards.

Once the page has been scanned, he uses a Wacom Cintiq monitor tablet and Adobe Photoshop to create separate layers to color on. The topmost layer is the black-and-white line art [Fig. A], and each character and major element gets its own layer so that the colors can

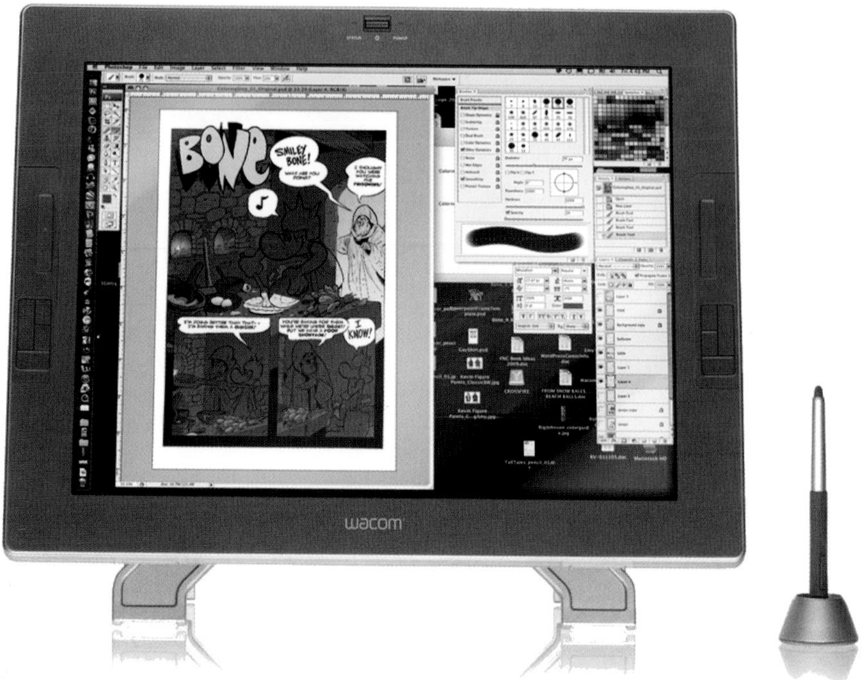
BONE
SMILEY BONE!
I KNOW!
wacom

be easily adjusted later [Fig. B]. For example, there are separate "Fone Bone" and "Thorn" layers for each page that those characters appear on. There is also a separate layer for the lettering [Fig. C]. Some pages can have many layers, depending on how complex they are.

Steve colors the background layers first and works his way up to the foreground. For instance, first the sky gets colored, followed by any trees, the ground, grass, the various characters, and so on. He blocks everything in solid colors first [Fig. D], then goes back and adds detail to each element [Fig. E]. He colors beneath the lines, and in some cases even colors the lines themselves – with smoke, for instance – to help "push" elements away from the panel's intended focus.

Areas of solid black in Jeff's original art are always kept as is. For example, sometimes Jeff uses black for

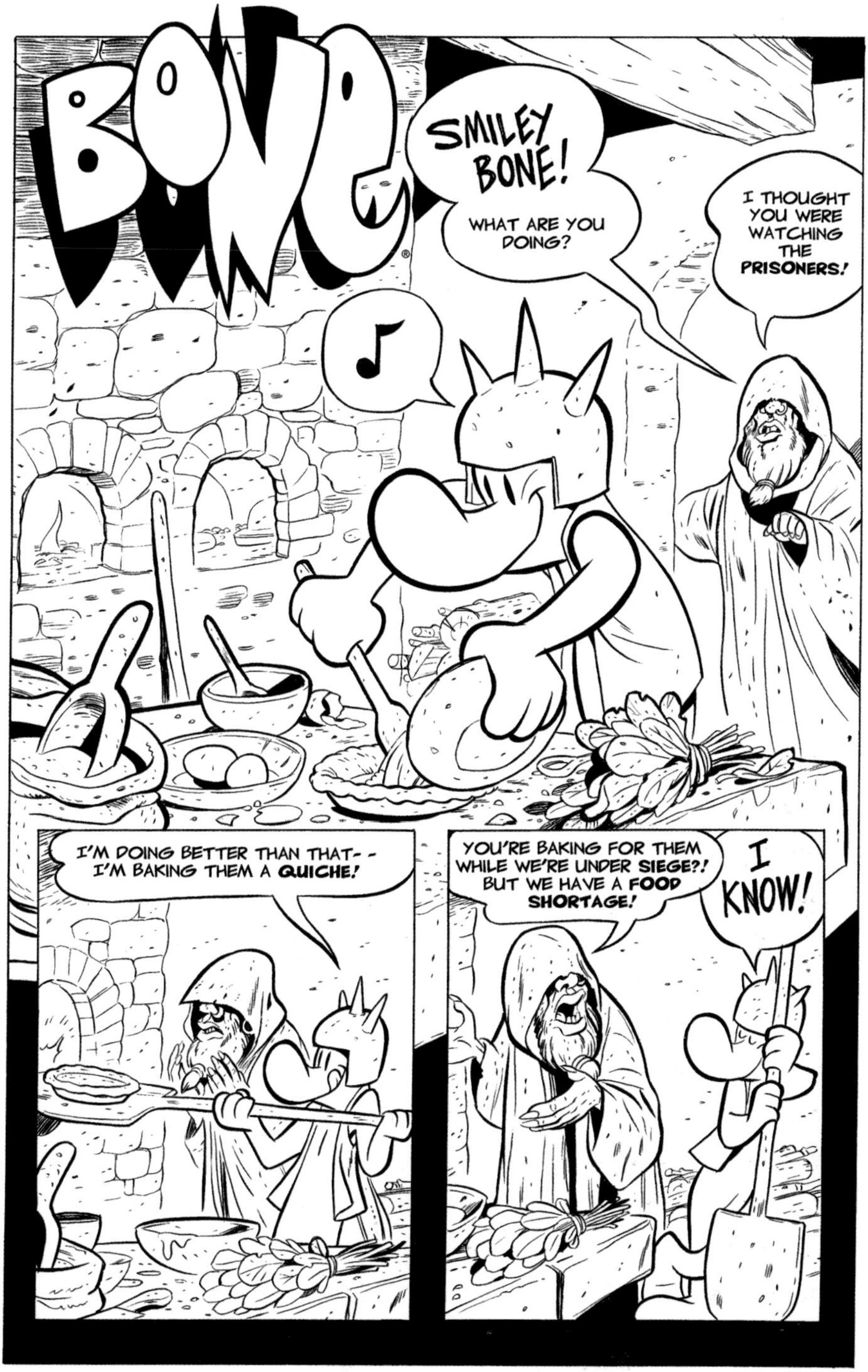
BONE®
SMILEY BONE!
WHAT ARE YOU DOING?
I THOUGHT YOU WERE WATCHING THE PRISONERS!
♪
I'M DOING BETTER THAN THAT- - I'M BAKING THEM A QUICHE!
YOU'RE BAKING FOR THEM WHILE WE'RE UNDER SIEGE?! BUT WE HAVE A FOOD SHORTAGE!
I KNOW!

A

objects in the background or extreme foreground, or for a shadow on a character's face. Steve never adds what he feels is unnecessary color to those elements.

Jeff and Steve always have a general discussion before final color decisions are made, so that they're in agreement about things like the time of day in a given scene. Once a color palette has been determined for the scene, the following pages are much easier to complete – until the setting changes again.

"Special effects" are kept to a minimum. Steve will sometimes add a little white airbrush glow to certain elements, such as burning candles or reflections in water (see the glow added around the oven flame, for instance), which adds a subtle feeling of realism. But he's always conscious of not overdoing these effects.

Once all the pages are colored, Jeff and Steve make changes based on how each scene reads to them. For instance, if their eyes are overly distracted by a particular element, they adjust the layers and balance the colors appropriately. After each page is approved by Jeff, Steve "flattens" it, compressing the multiple layers into a single layer. He then copies the files to a hard drive, which is sent to Scholastic for the final page layout and design.

FUN FACT: Did you know that the Bone cousins' forefather, Big Johnson Bone, is the fabled boogeyman known as the "Jekk" that the Rat Creatures fear? He came to the Valley many, many years before the Bone cousins, and fought the Rat Creatures by swinging them around by their tails.

B

C

D

E

A CONVERSATION WITH STEVE HAMAKER

Steve Hamaker has worked closely with Jeff since 1998 and took on the job of coloring all 1,300 pages of **BONE**, *earning three Eisner Award nominations along the way. Steve gave us the opportunity to ask him a few questions – take a look at what he had to say!*

Did you read comics and watch cartoons as a kid?

I did! I loved a lot of older cartoons when I was a kid, like *The Flintstones, Scooby-Doo,* all of the Chuck Jones –directed Looney Toons cartoons, and Woody Wood-pecker was a big favorite. With comic books, I loved the original *Teenage Mutant Ninja Turtles.* Even as a kid I knew that the creators of *TMNT* were self-publishers, like Jeff Smith was later, and that made a huge impres-sion on me to make my own comics!

When did you know you wanted to be an artist? Did anything happen that helped make up your mind?

I knew from about the age of three that I would draw my whole life. I never expected to make a living at it, but the desire to create art has always been with me. My mom and dad were very supportive from the start, and if they hadn't been, I would certainly not have made a successful career out of my art.

What kind of art did you study at Columbus College of Art & Design? What kind of work did you anticipate doing after graduating?

I was an illustration major. I went to that college in pursuit of a job with Disney as an animator or storyboard artist. I quickly changed the focus of my goals to comics and painting because the animation department seemed too focused on just one aspect of art for the students interested in getting Disney internships.

When you were younger, did you ever get in trouble for drawing in school when you weren't supposed to be?

I went to public school, so yes, there were many times when I was asked to stop drawing during class. However, when I was in fourth through sixth grades, I was in a public school program that encouraged creative thinking and art. We had weekly art classes at the Flint Institute of Arts and I was encouraged to use my drawing abilities in many school projects. That really helped me understand that art was a great thing for learning, so having an outlet within the classroom was amazing. My teachers there encouraged me to draw, but I still tried to sneak in some doodling while they were talking. Ha-ha!

If you could draw yourself as a character in BONE, what kind of character would you be?

Maybe tall like Smiley, but with glasses and a baseball cap! I would definitely wear pants, though.

Was there anything regarding the coloring that you and Jeff had a difference of opinion over?

We never had any big disagreements. Small things, like what color Thorn's cape should be; but most of the time we would come up with cool reasons why clothing would change from scene to scene, or book to book. Most of my ideas were actually okay by him. As long as I had a good story reason, he would go for it.

Can you give us any insights into conversations you had with Jeff about specific coloring choices – perhaps for one of the characters or one of the settings?

I was very interested in making the corrupted stick-eaters in Atheia all have brighter-colored robes. The high-ranking officers would have green and yellow robes, whereas the soldiers would be in purple and red. Just giving them a different color than the good stick-eaters was important to me; since they had strayed away from the rest, maybe the colors could show us that. Jeff agreed. Also, I colored the leader, Tarsil, in more traditional red robes, because he's the kind of person who would never forget that the Dragons scarred him years before, and the Red Dragon color scheme influenced his outfit. That was a fun way of giving a little background depth to those characters.

Which was your favorite character to color? The most difficult?

I loved coloring Kingdok and the Hooded One! Thorn was usually the most difficult, but she always looked the nicest when I was finished! The Bones were harder than you might think. It's very easy to over-render them, and we made sure they were always very simple and cartoony compared to the other characters and settings.

One of the stupid, stupid Rat Creatures likes quiche, and the other insists on stew. What's your favorite food?

Currently my favorite snack food is fried pickles! That might sound strange, but believe me, they are amazing! Otherwise, I love a good burger or a sub.

What do you like to do when you're not coloring?

I play a lot of computer games to unwind at home, and of course I never stopped loving cartoons! I create and publish my own comics when I get the time as well! A few years ago I self-published a book called *Fish N Chips* about a cat and fish superhero team that fights vampires. I also do webcomics occasionally about my online video game characters [which can be found at www.steve-hamaker.com].

You've mentioned that you probably would have colored the first volumes of the series differently based on what you've learned working on the succeeding volumes. What changes would you go back and make if you had the opportunity?

I would color those scenes differently now, yes; but if I was given the chance to change them, I wouldn't. I have a strong belief that artists should let go of their work after some time. Most artists would agree that it's difficult to know when to stop. In the case of my coloring on *BONE*, I feel like I did improve as I went along. However, I like seeing that progression because it seems to fit the theme of the series itself. The characters all go through changes, so in a way the coloring grows with them. If I found mistakes then I would change things, but I was confident when I finished those earlier books, so I remain satisfied with my work on the whole.

Is there one particular page or scene in all the *BONE* volumes that stands out as a favorite of yours?

It would be a tie between the cow race [book two] and the Phoney Bone balloon scene [book six, page 111]. The cow race is just so funny, but very complicated, so I was happy with how it turned out. The dramatic lighting was a lot of fun in the Phoney Bone balloon scene.

How do you feel your coloring has changed the *BONE* experience for readers?

I have heard many people say that they found it easier to get younger kids to read *BONE* after it appeared in color, so that is a nice thing. Jeff had success with a wide range of ages when it was in black and white, so I don't consider the colored books superior or anything like that. I was a fan of many black-and-white comics as a very young kid, so I think it's just a matter of personal preference. The biggest measure of success for me is if Jeff likes the color, because he created the story and he knows how it should look!

COVER GALLERY

Before *BONE* was published at Scholastic, it was self-published as single-issue comics by Cartoon Books. Have a look at some of the cover art for those original editions!

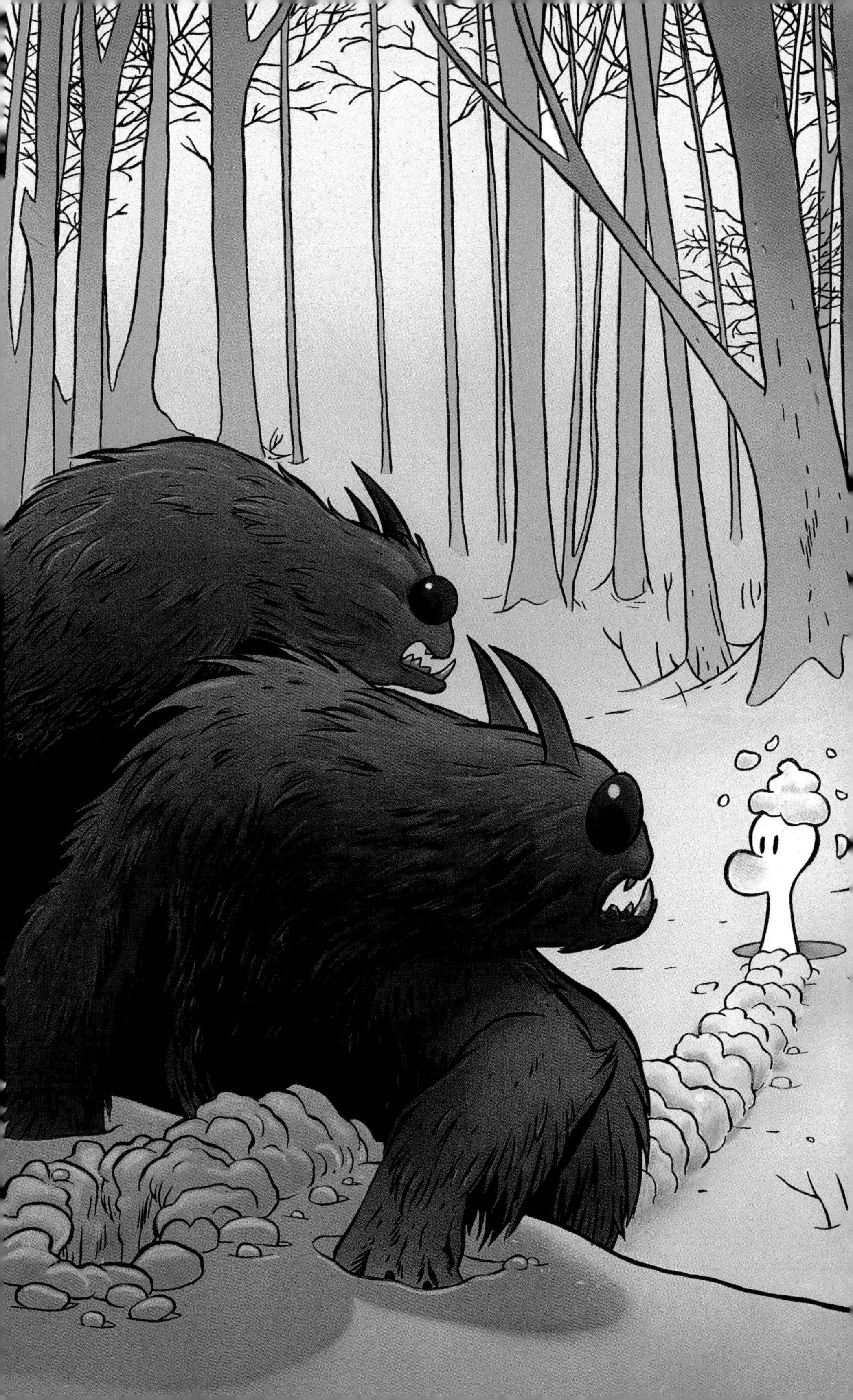

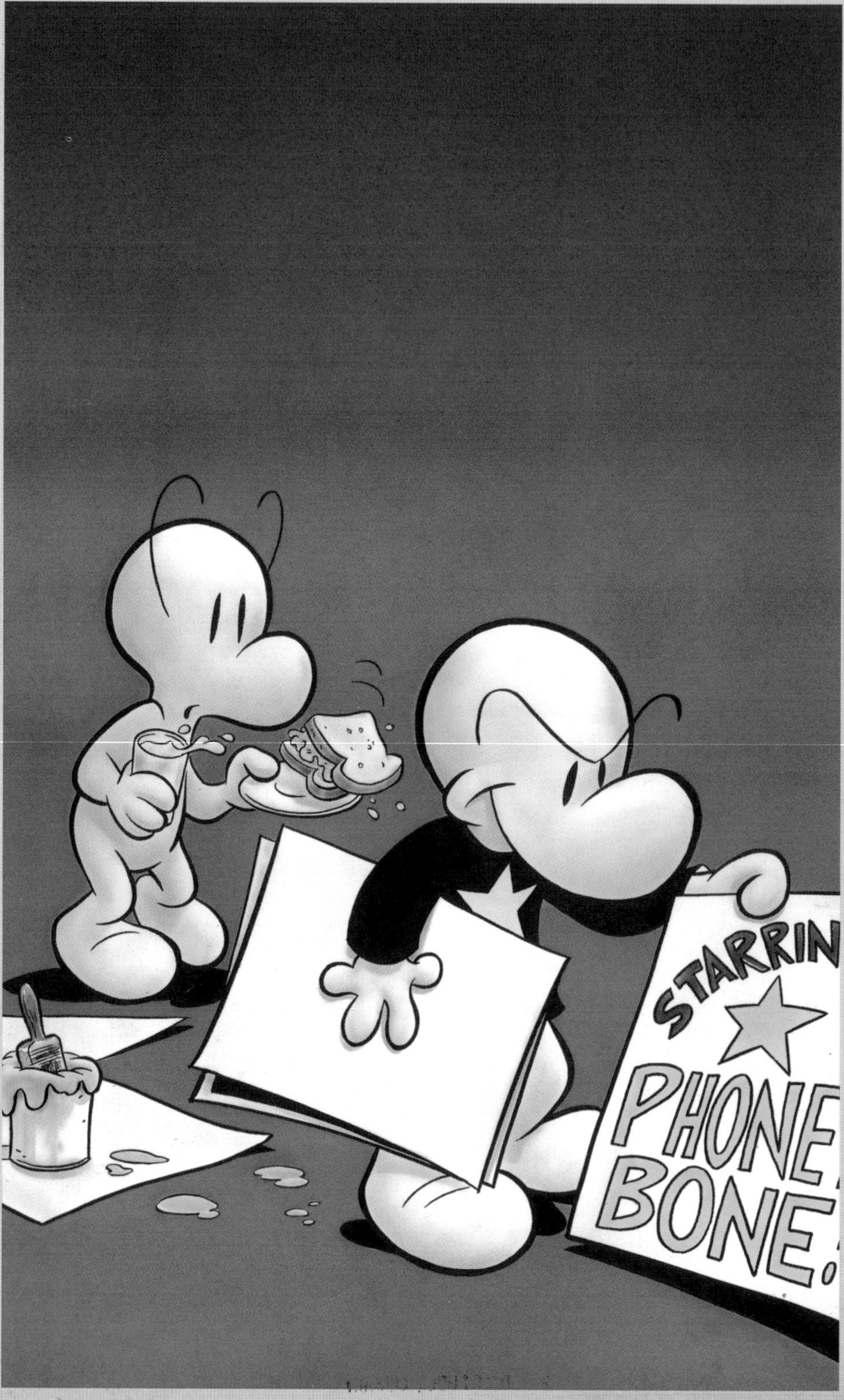
STARRIN
PHONE
BONE

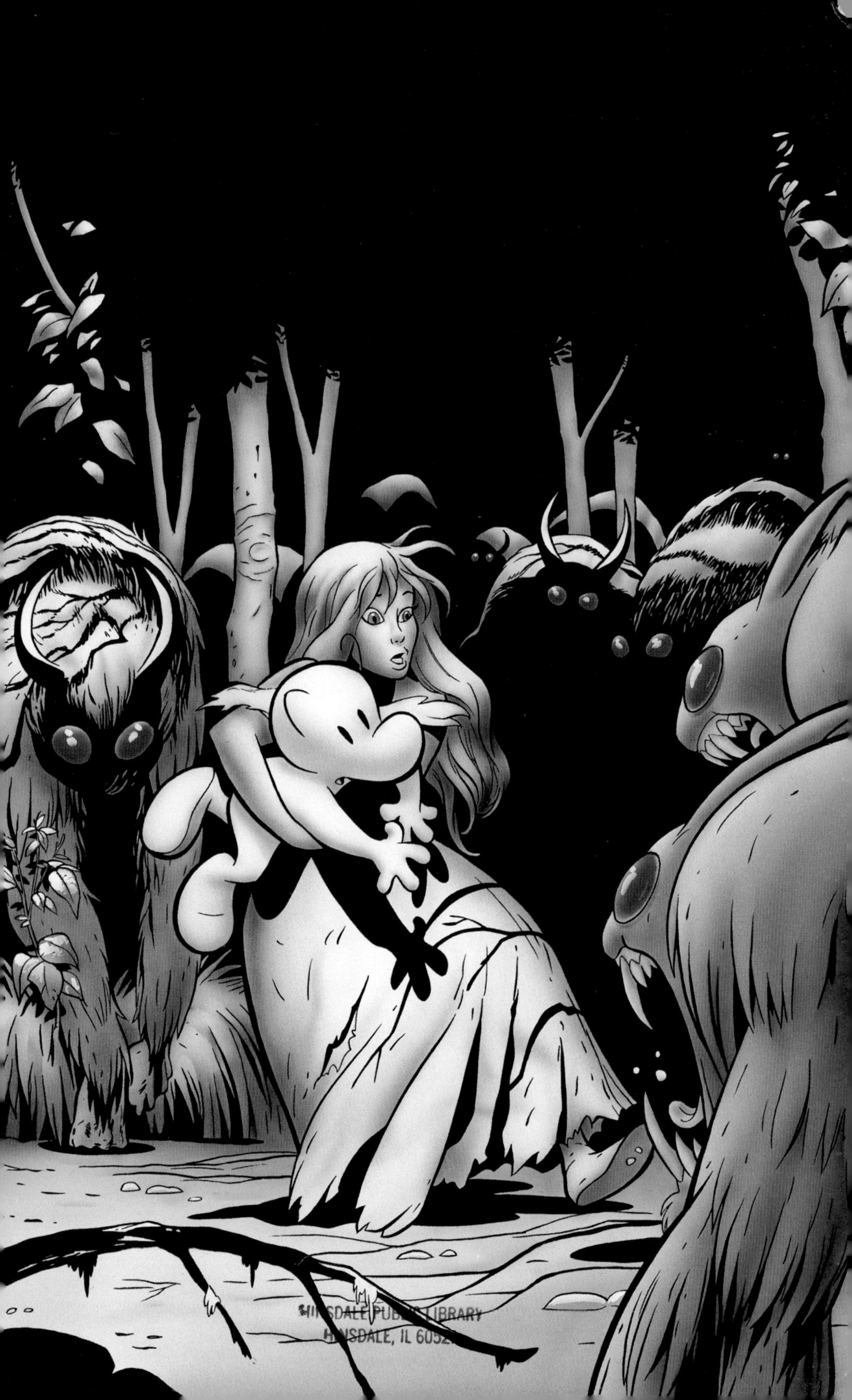

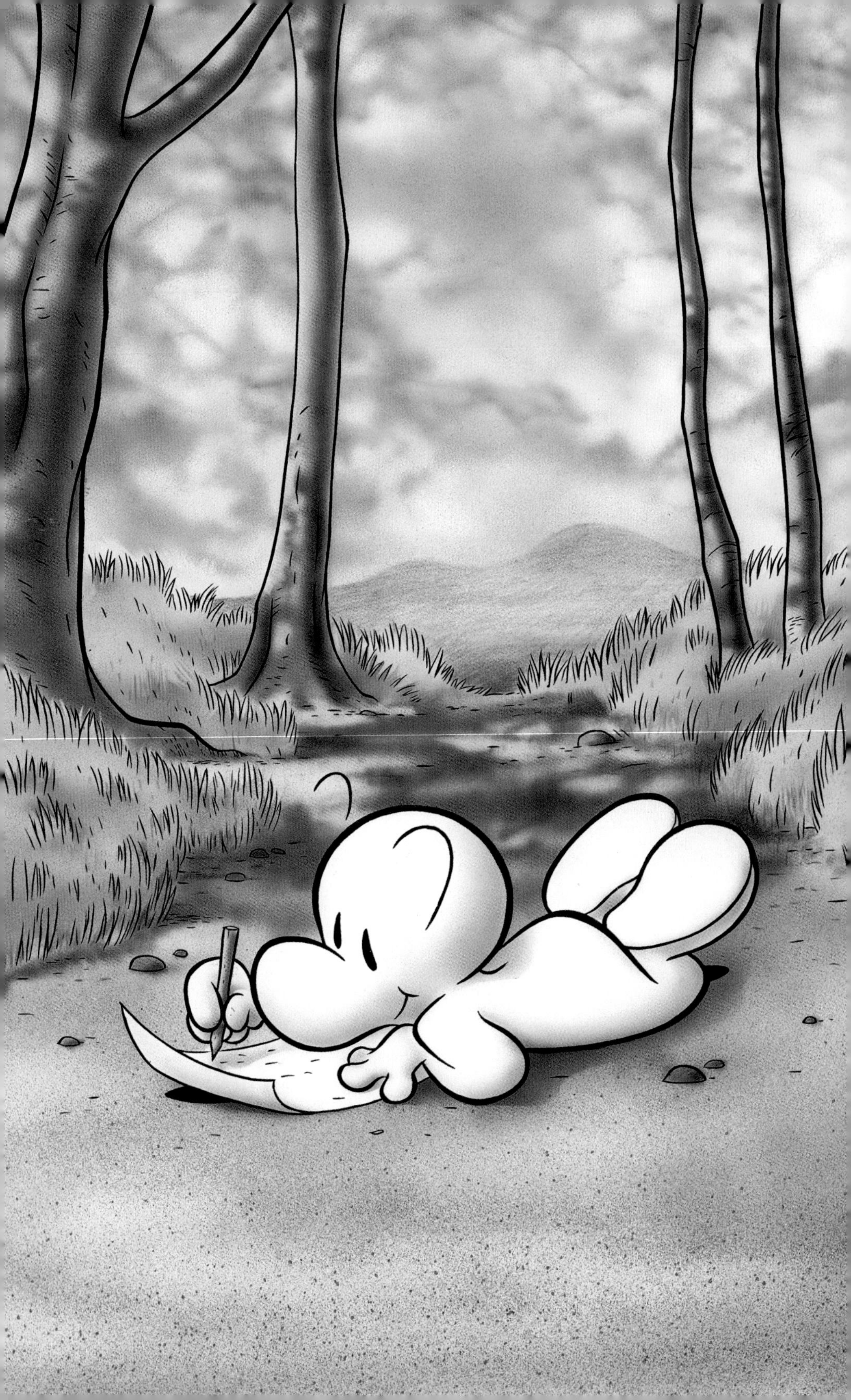

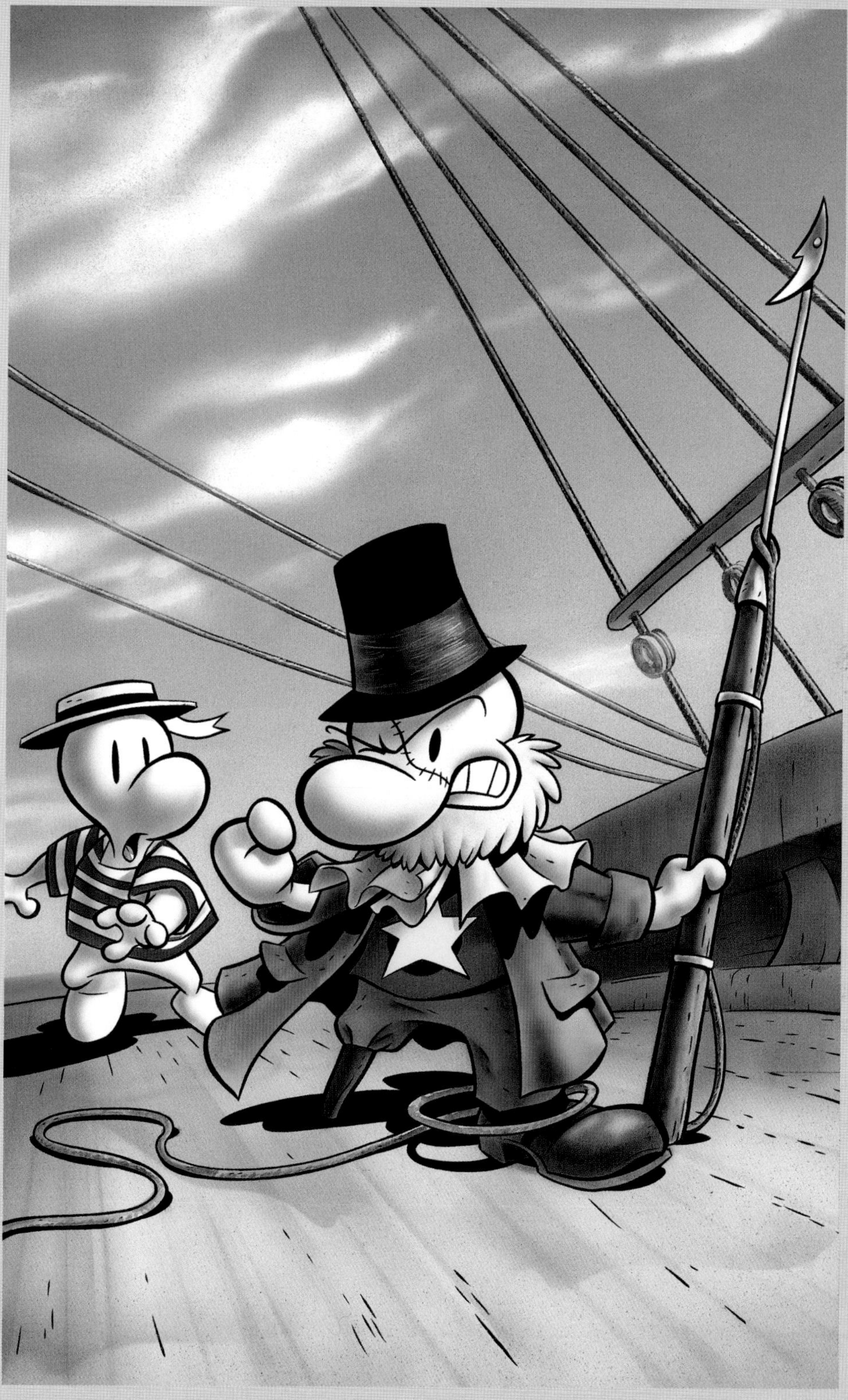

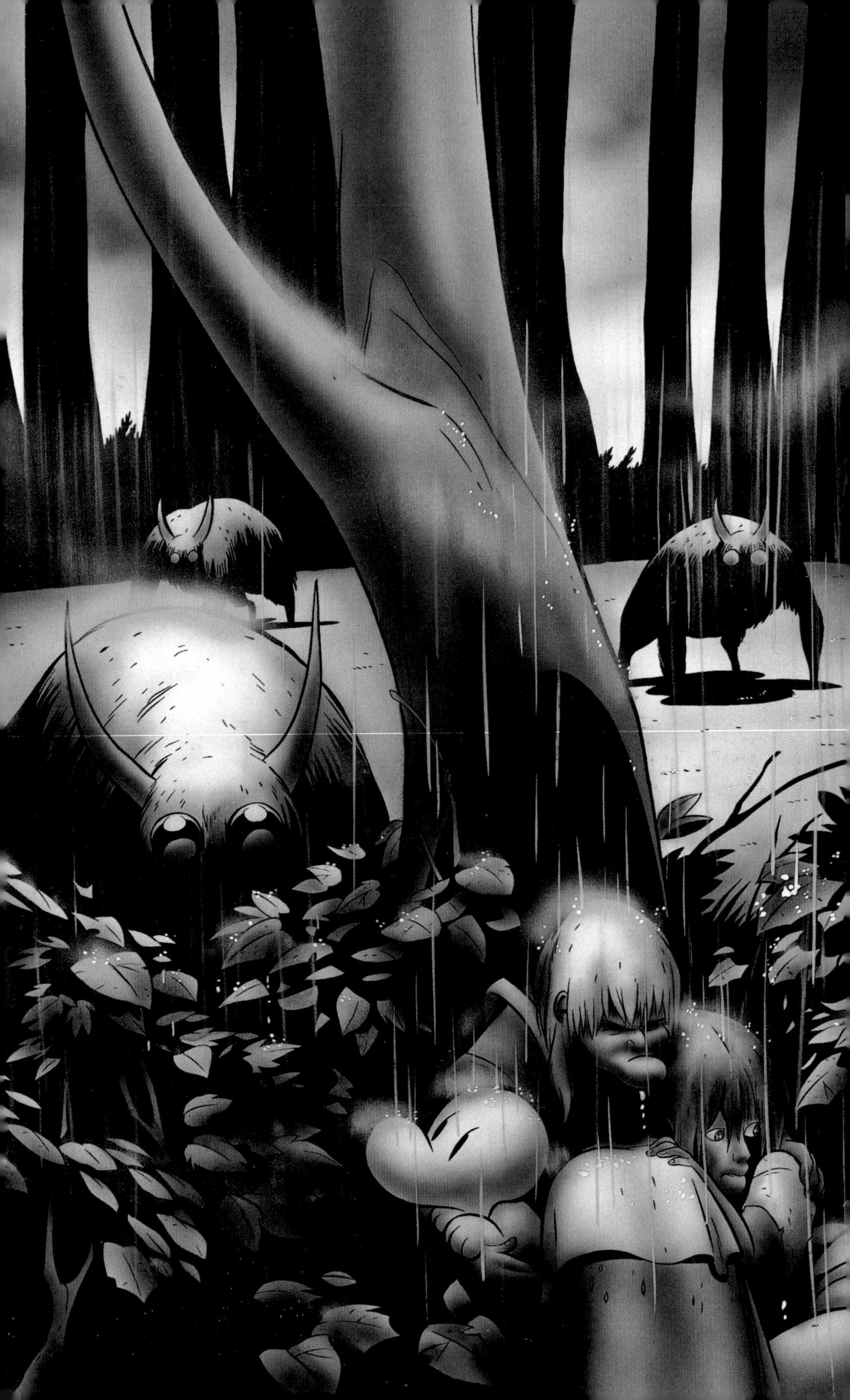

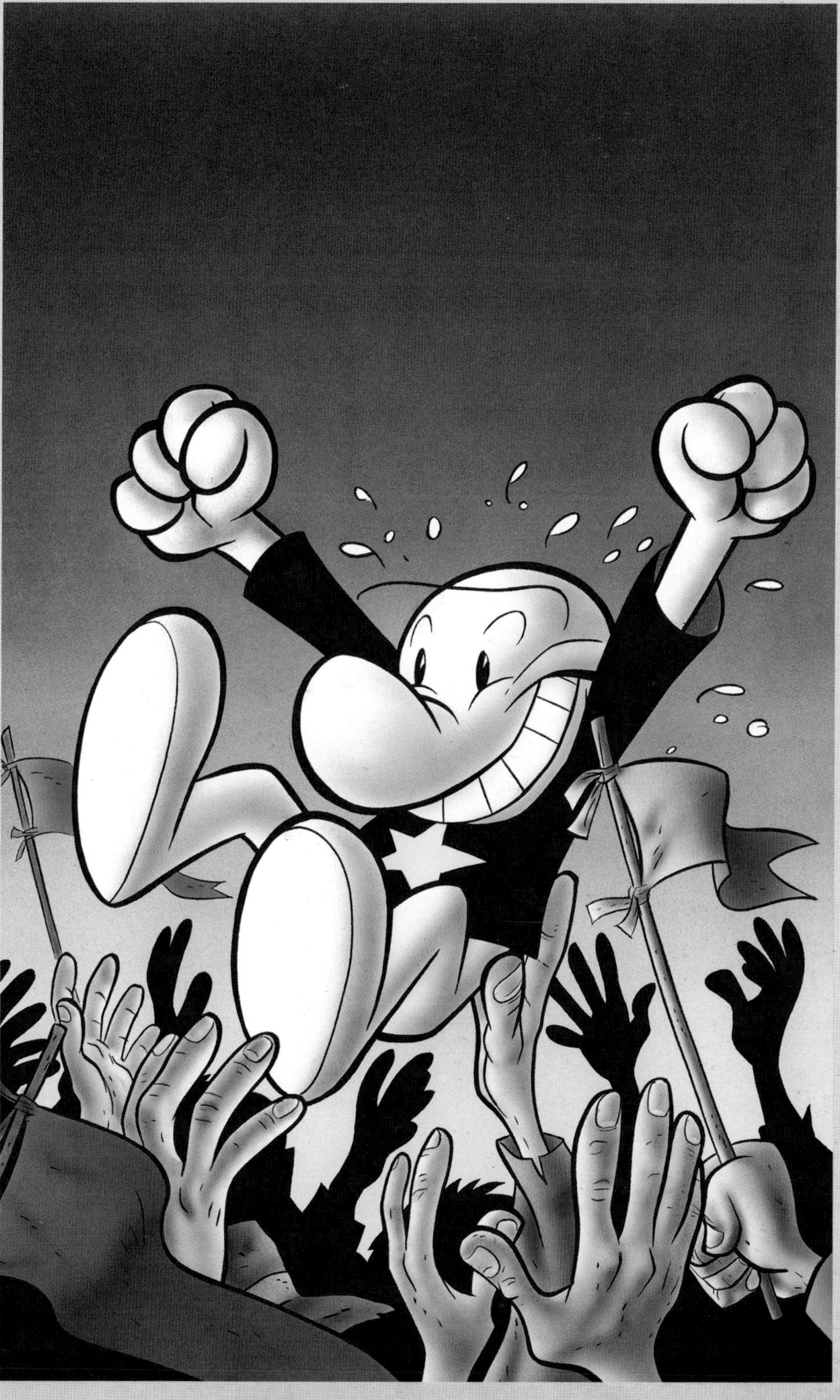

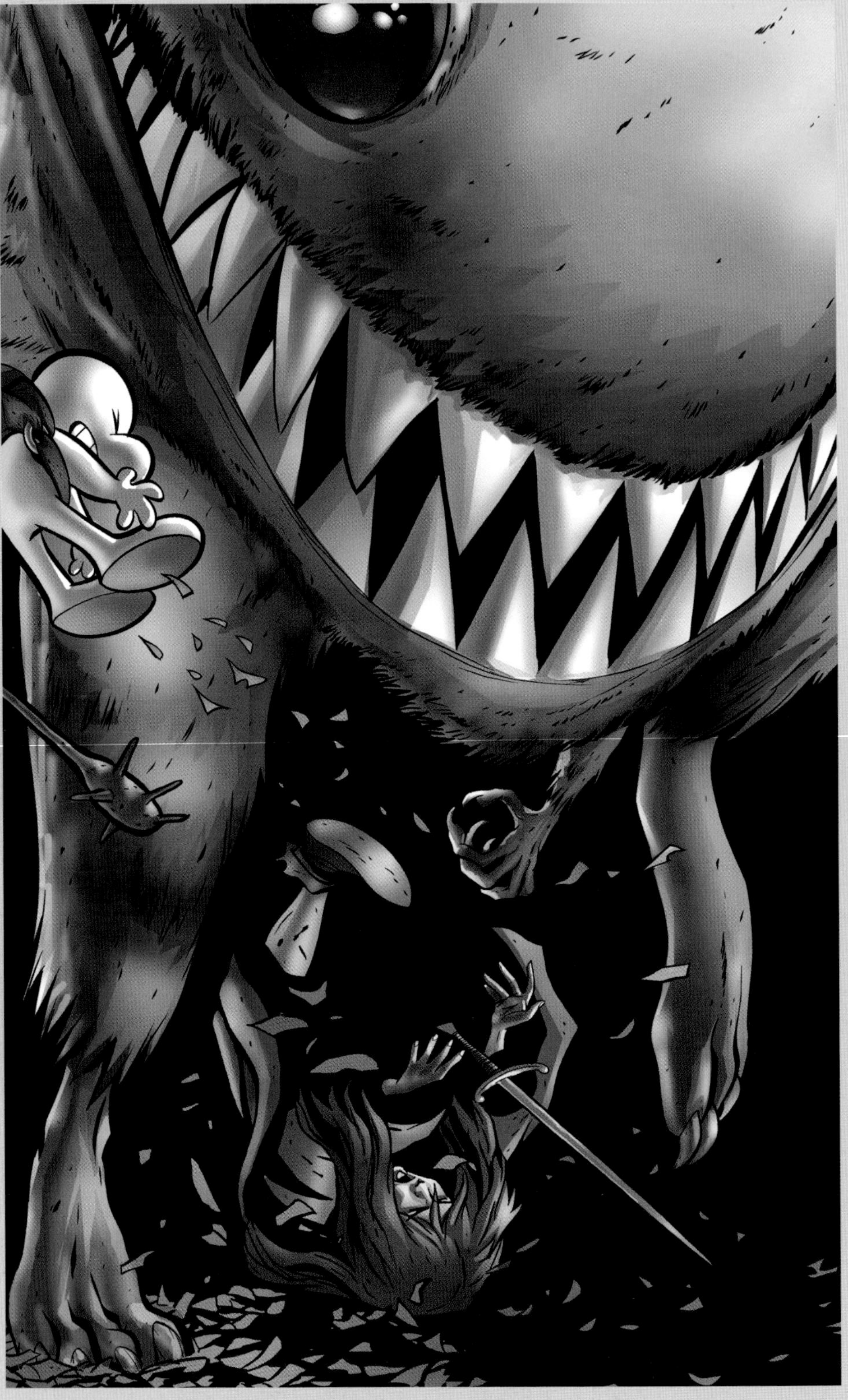

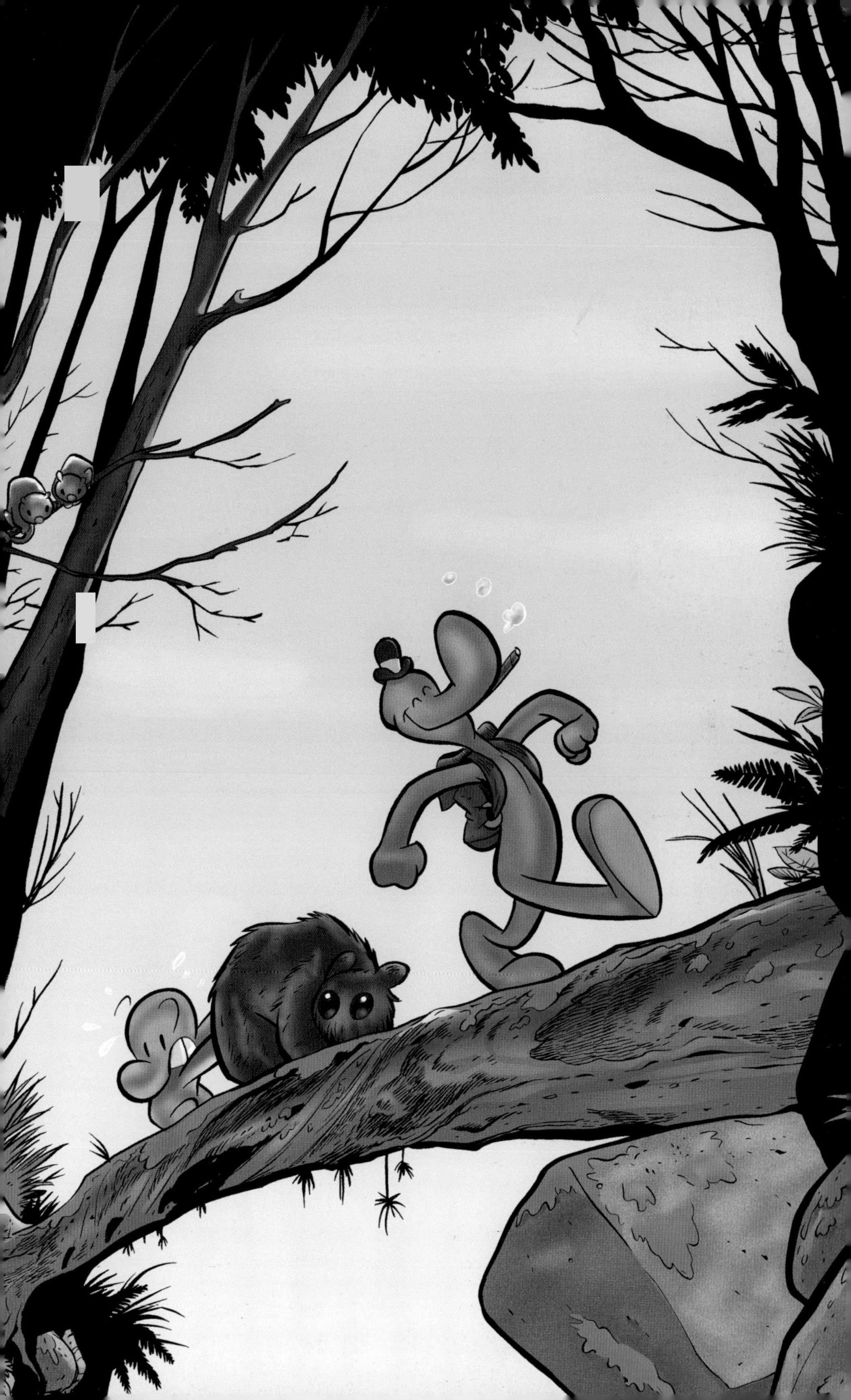

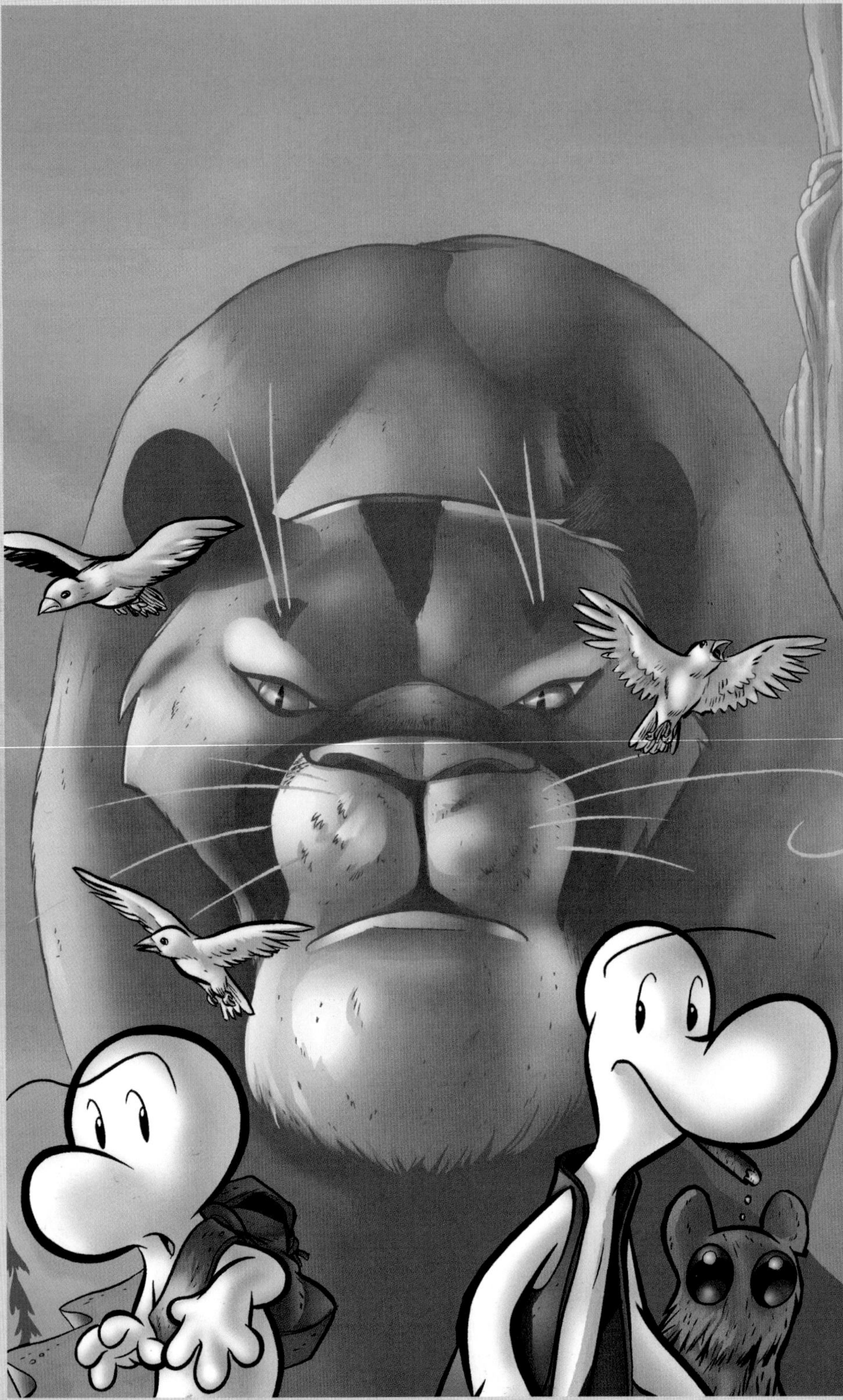

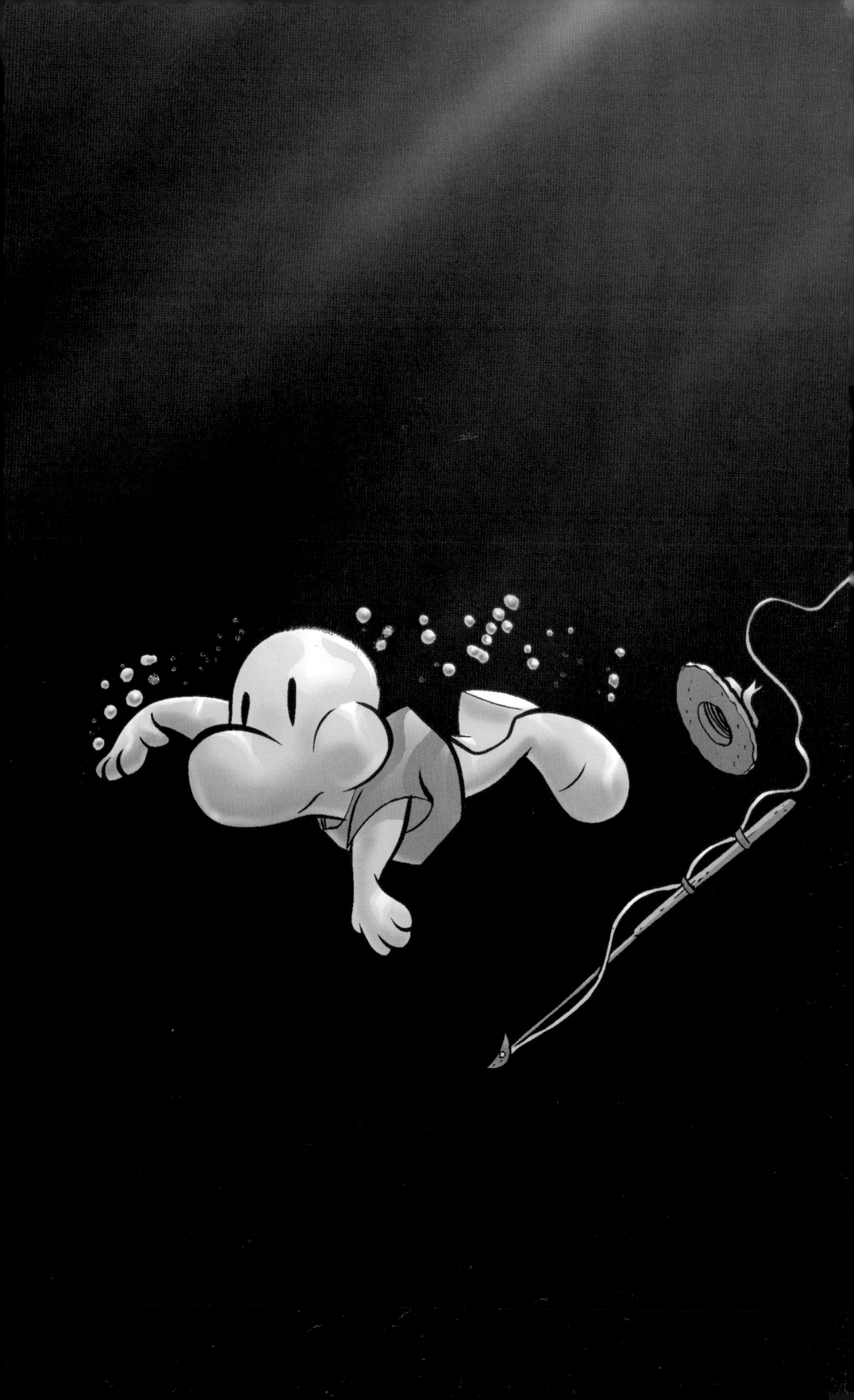

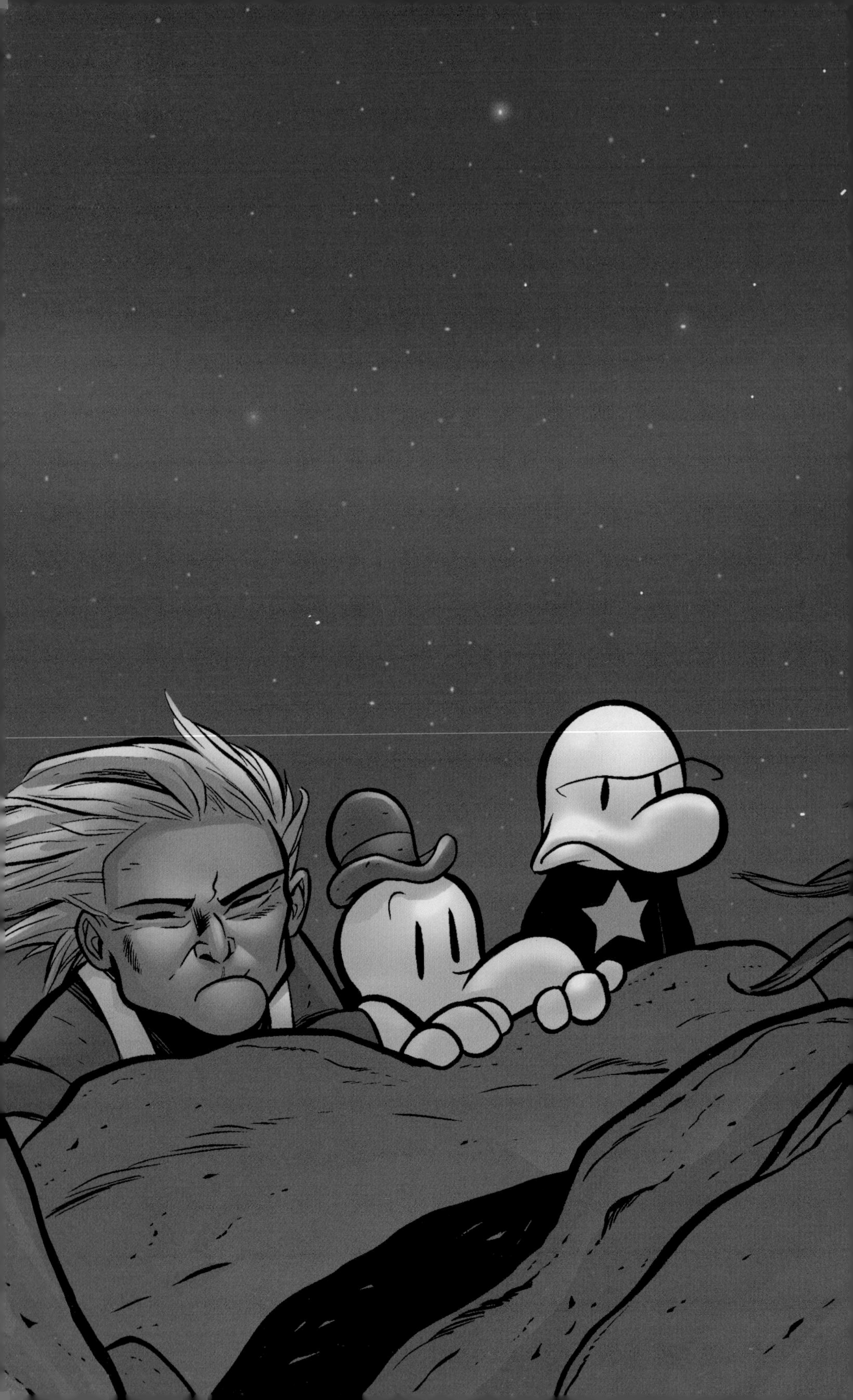

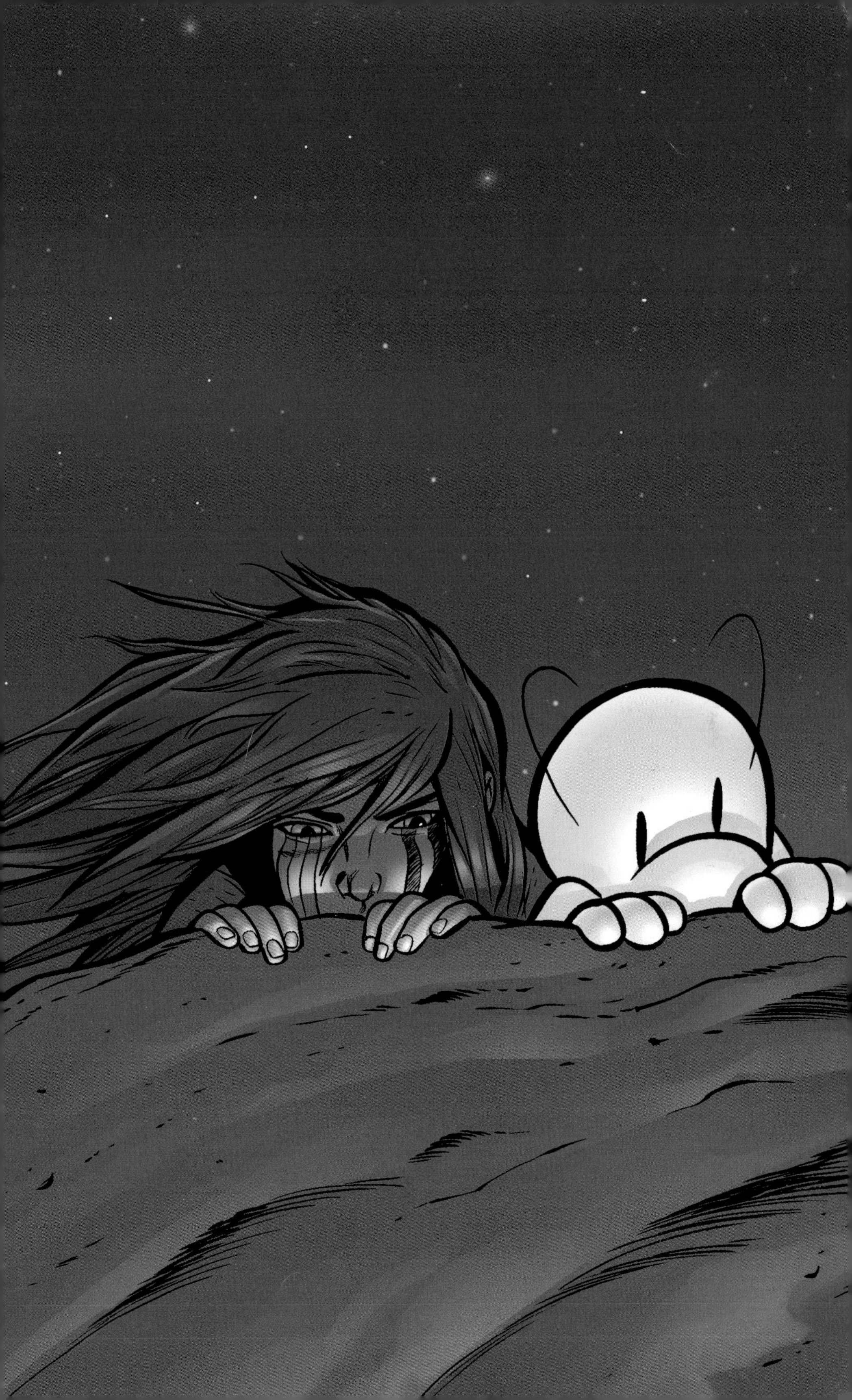

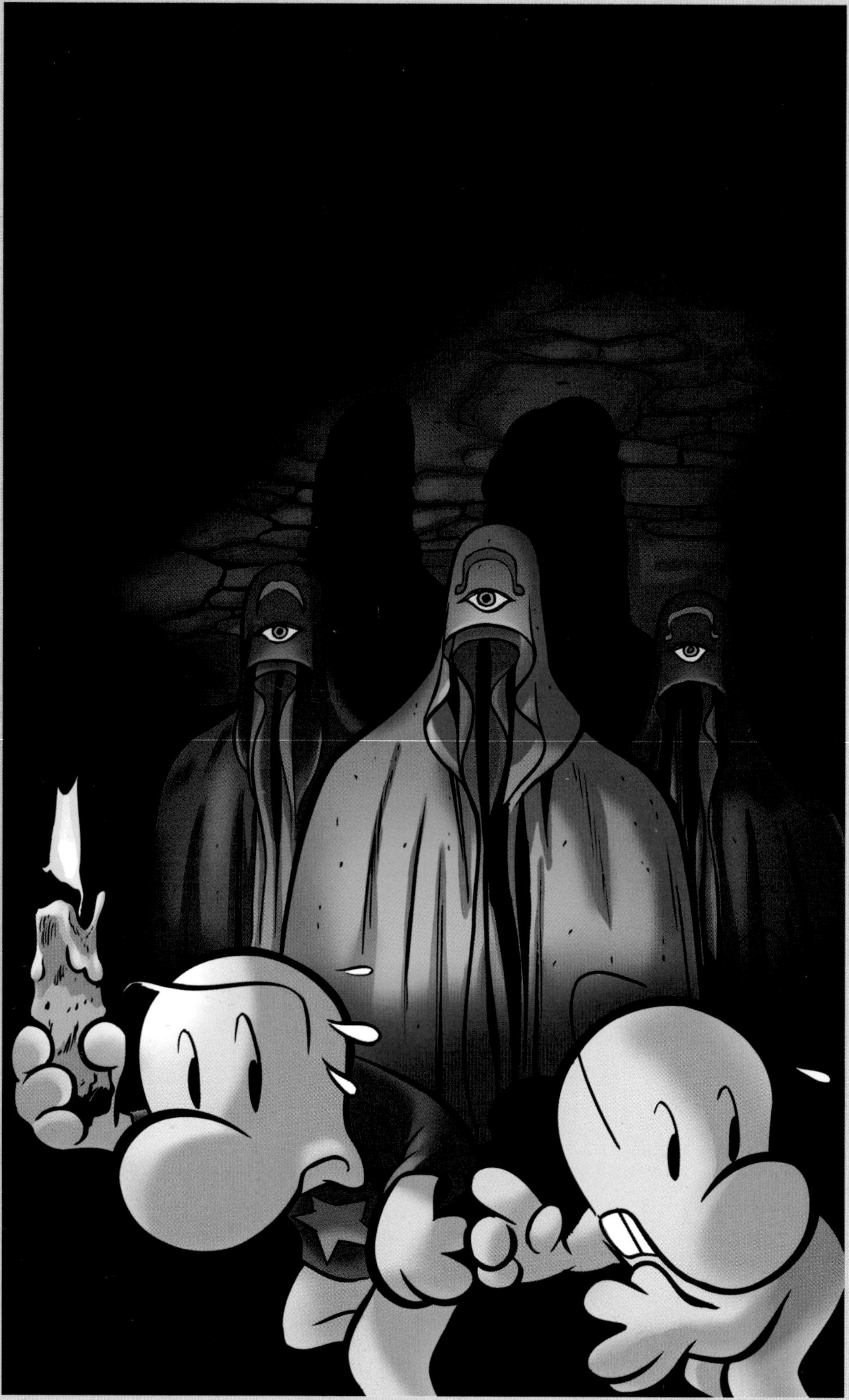

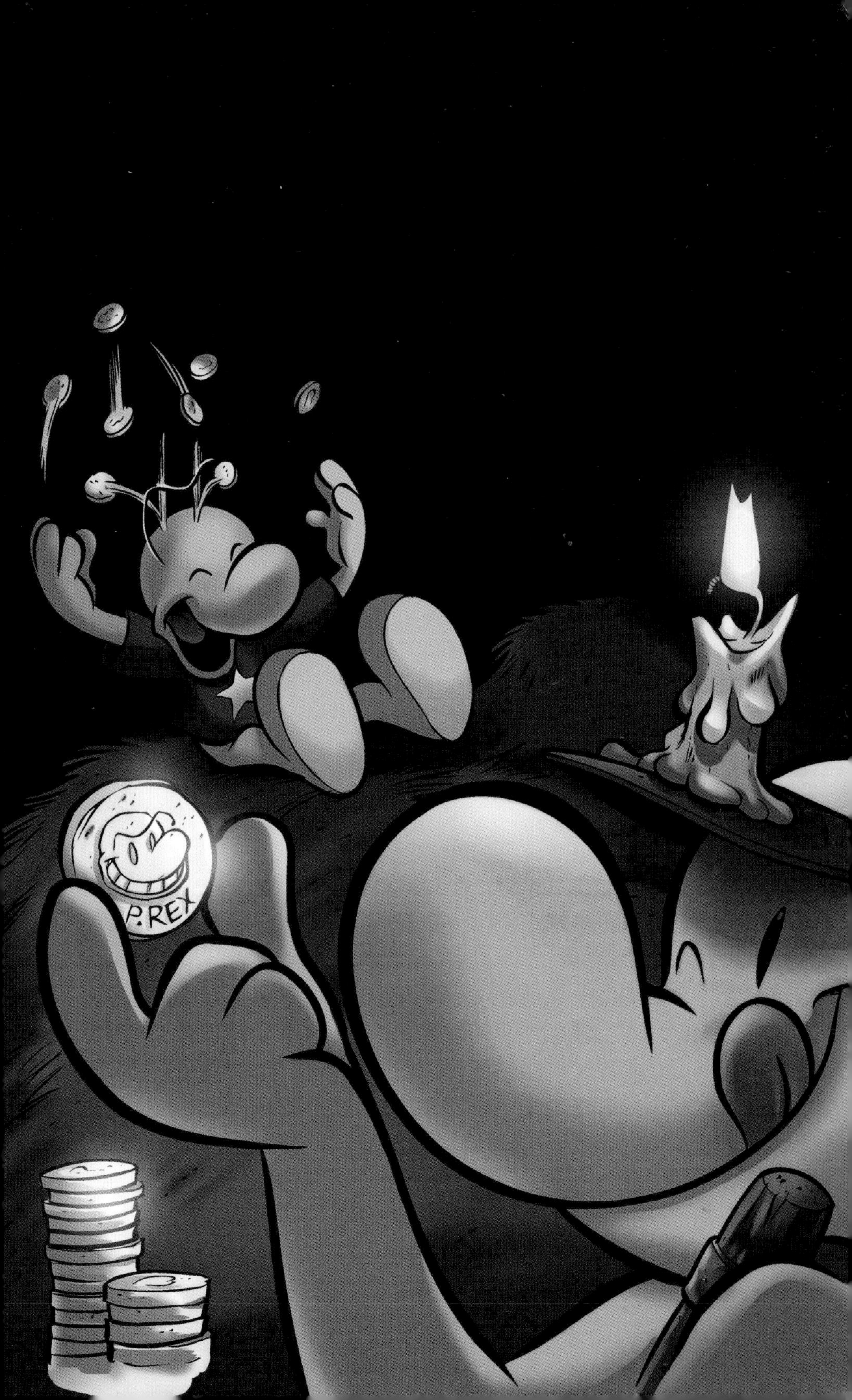
P.REX

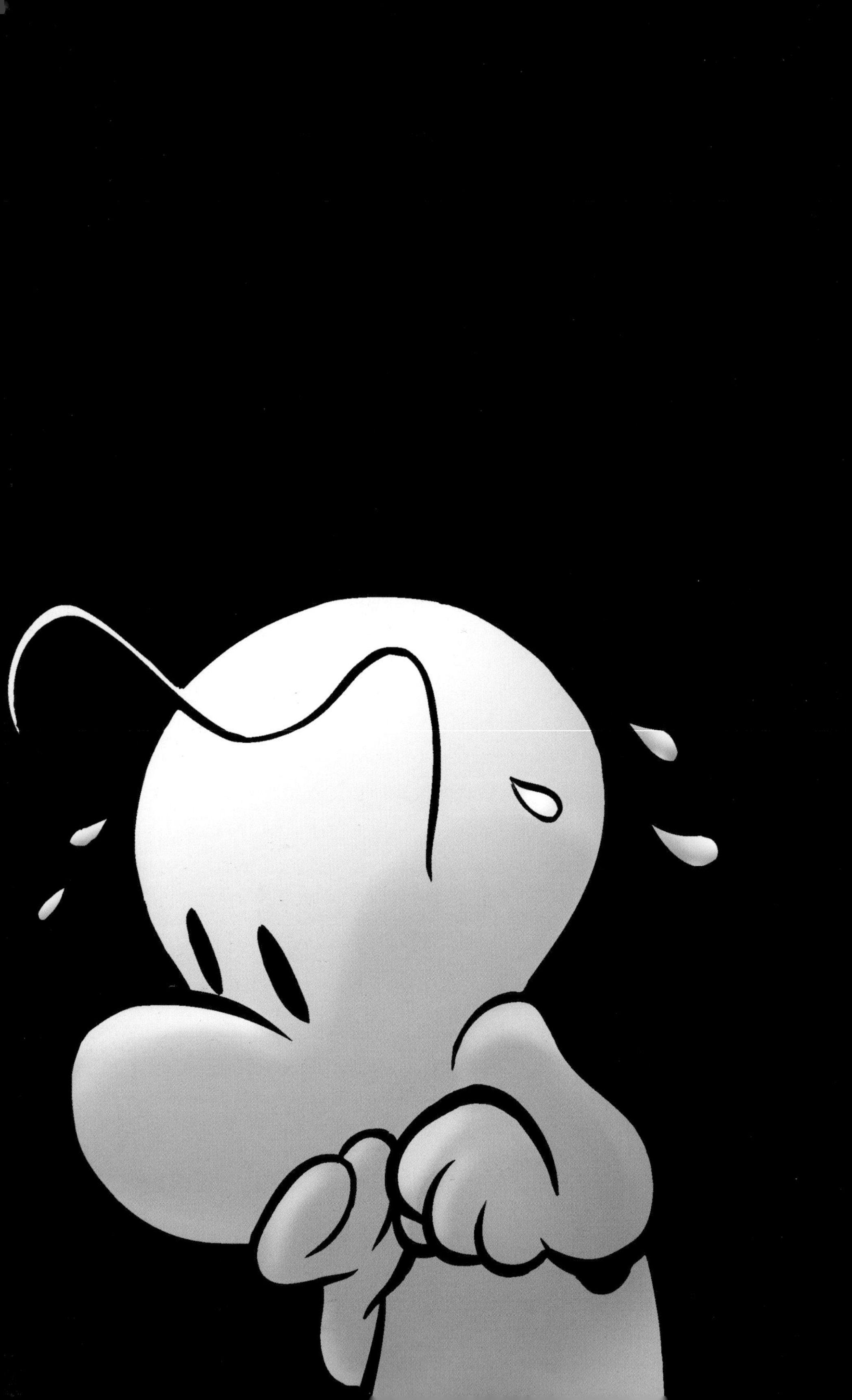

COVER INDEX

ISSUE #2
SEPT 1991

ISSUE #16
OCT 1994

ISSUE #39
OCT 2000

ISSUE #3
DEC 1991

ISSUE #19
JUNE 1995

ISSUE #40
JAN 2001

ISSUE #5
JUNE 1992

ISSUE #21
DEC 1995

ISSUE #45
NOV 2001

ISSUE #11
DEC 1993

ISSUE #29
NOV 1997

ISSUE #47
MAY 2002

ISSUE #13
MARCH 1994

ISSUE #31
APRIL 1998

ISSUE #50
DEC 2002

GLOSSARY

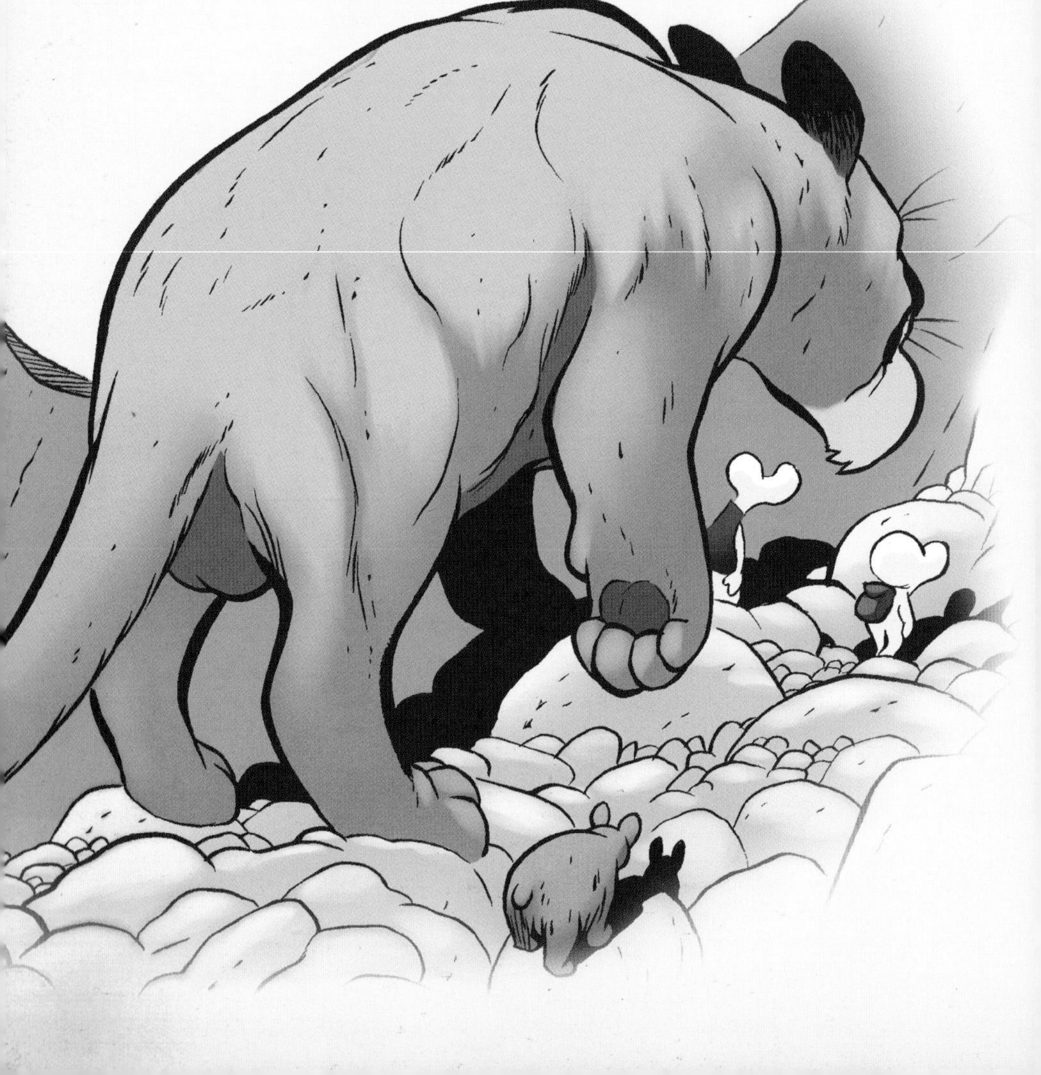

Atheia

A walled city located at the southern end of the Valley. It is the traditional seat of the Kingdom of Atheia and home to the Atheian royal family.

Barrelhaven

A village in the northern part of the Valley. It's the site of the Valley's annual Spring Fair, held at the local fairgrounds.

Barrelhaven Tavern

An inn located in the center of Barrelhaven, with a bar downstairs and rooms to rent upstairs. It's owned and operated by Lucius Down.

Blank Sandwich

A favorite meal of Smiley's: two slices of bread with nothing in between. The Bone cousins ate them as young orphans in Boneville.

Boneville

The home of the Bone cousins. Although Boneville is never actually seen in the story, Fone Bone refers to its extensive downtown, Phoney carries bills of the local currency, and Smiley talks about the presence of nuclear reactors and a CornDogHut.

Conkle's Hollow

Situated midway between Old Man's Cave and the Eastern Mountains, a bridge crosses the river here on the road to Oak Bottom.

Crown of Horns
A massive, gold-infused structure of stalagmites inside a cavern at Tanen Gard. It sits directly on the "veil," half in the real world and half in the Dreaming, serving as the point of balance between the two worlds.

Deren Gard
A Dragon lair situated on a cliff overlooking the northern Valley. During the Great War, five-year-old Thorn was hidden here.

Dragon's Stair
A mountain pass near Deren Gard where Phoney and the Barrelhaven townsfolk attempt to trap the Red Dragon.

Dreaming
Believed by most Valley dwellers to be the source of life itself. Also referred to as the "Old Time" (by Thorn), the "Venscape" (by the Veni Yan), and the "Hum-Hum" (by the animals of the Valley).

Dreaming Eye
The point where the Dreaming flows through living beings. Some Dreaming eyes are stronger than others, and some aren't open at all.

Eastern Mountains
A mountain range extending along the entire eastern edge of the Valley. Rock Jaw roams primarily in the northern section of these mountains.

Eggs

The primary currency used in most of the Valley. Atheians explain to Phoney that eggs are used only "out in the sticks"; in Atheia, gold is the preferred currency.

Flat-landers

The term used by Kingdok and the Rat Creatures for humans living in the Valley.

Flint Ridge

A large outcropping of rock in the southern Valley, overlooking the Great Basin.

Ghost Circles

Illusions that are part of the Dreaming where there is no shape or form – only void and nothingness – and appear where the real world and the void are mixed together. The boundaries of a ghost circle are invisible to everyone except those who have a strong connection to the Dreaming.

Gitchy

A strange, tingling feeling that Gran'ma Ben gets that warns her of bad things to come. It can vary in intensity, but it's never wrong!

Great Basin

A large lowland area in the southern Valley between Tanen Gard and Flint Ridge.

Great Cow Race
An annual event held at Barrelhaven's Spring Fair, in which Gran'ma Ben races against the Valley's prize racing cows.

Great War
A war fought approximately fifteen years prior to the events in *BONE* between the humans of the Valley and the Rat Creatures. Also referred to as the "Big War."

High Council
The ruling body of the Dragons. (The Rat Creatures also hold what they refer to as a "high council," presided over alternately by Kingdok and the Hooded One.)

Inner Council
The governing body of Atheia. It was dissolved and replaced by the Vedu when they took over the city.

Knott's Defeat
A clearing in the Valley midway between Old Man's Cave and Flint Ridge.

Midsummer Picnic
An annual affair in Barrelhaven for which the townspeople hoard goods all year long in anticipation.

Moby Dick
A classic novel by Herman Melville about a hunt for a great white whale. Fone Bone's favorite book; he brought a copy with him from Boneville.

Mystery Cow
Smiley Bone entered the Great Cow Race as the "Mystery Cow," dressed in a big-headed cow costume, with the intent to help Phoney fix the race.

Nessen
An ancient Rat Creature military language.

Nights of Lightning
A series of vicious, brutal attacks by Rat Creatures on the humans in the Valley during the Great War.

Old Man's Cave
A large and beautiful cave to the east of Barrel-haven where the Veni Yan Monks are trained. This is believed to be the place where Ven received the wisdom of the Dreaming from the Dragons. Gran'ma Ben calls Old Man's Cave the "center of all that is transcendent in this world."

Pawa
A territory in the southeastern part of the Valley. The Pawans are allied with the Rat Creatures and the Hooded One against their Atheian neighbors.

Pawa Road
A road leading from Atheia in the south to Pawa in the east.

Prayer Stone
A stone inscribed with devotional words or designs. Atheians believe carving a prayer into stone gives it strength and permanence.

Prayer Stone Hill
A place near Tanen Guard where a group of large prayer stones are arrayed. Atheians bury prayer stones there, believing their prayers will be delivered directly to the Dragons living underground.

Sinner's Rock
A large rock outcropping just west of Atheia, connected to the city via a secret tunnel. It's the scene of one of the climactic battles between the Pawan and Rat Creature armies and the Atheian forces led by Gran'ma Ben.

Spring Fair
An annual event in Barrelhaven that Thorn looks forward to with great anticipation. It features dozens of vendor's booths, such as honey sellers, and the highlight of the fair – the Great Cow Race.

Stony Gulch
A long, deep ravine running along the entire west side of the Valley.

Tanen Gard

The bottomless gorge that serves as the sacred burial grounds of the Dragons and the location of the Crown of Horns.

Turning

The point at which a Veni Yan Cari awakens to his or her abilities.

Valley

The Valley encompasses the vast area running from the cliffs of Deren Gard in the north to Atheia in the south, with Stony Gulch and the Eastern Mountains making up its western and eastern borders, respectively. Compared to Boneville, the Valley is relatively medieval, judging by its lifestyle, weapons, and modes of transportation. Phoney Bone, in fact, refers to the Valley people as "yokels."

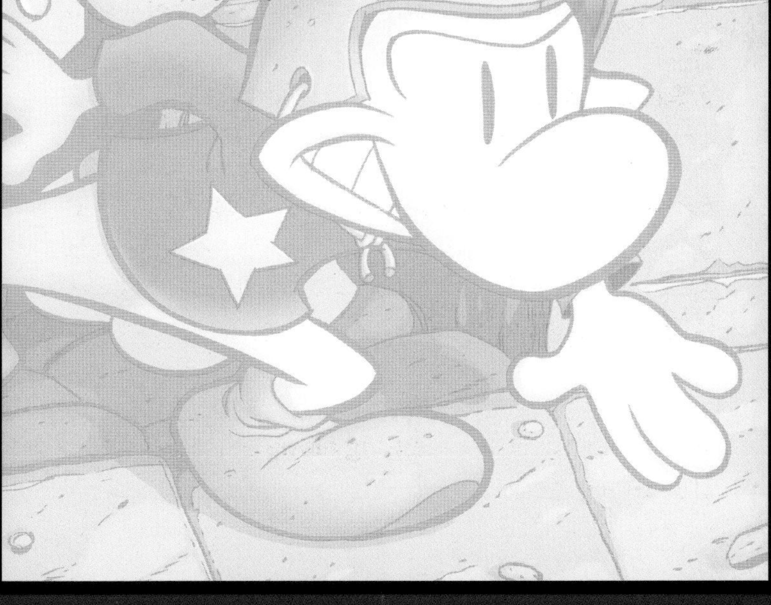

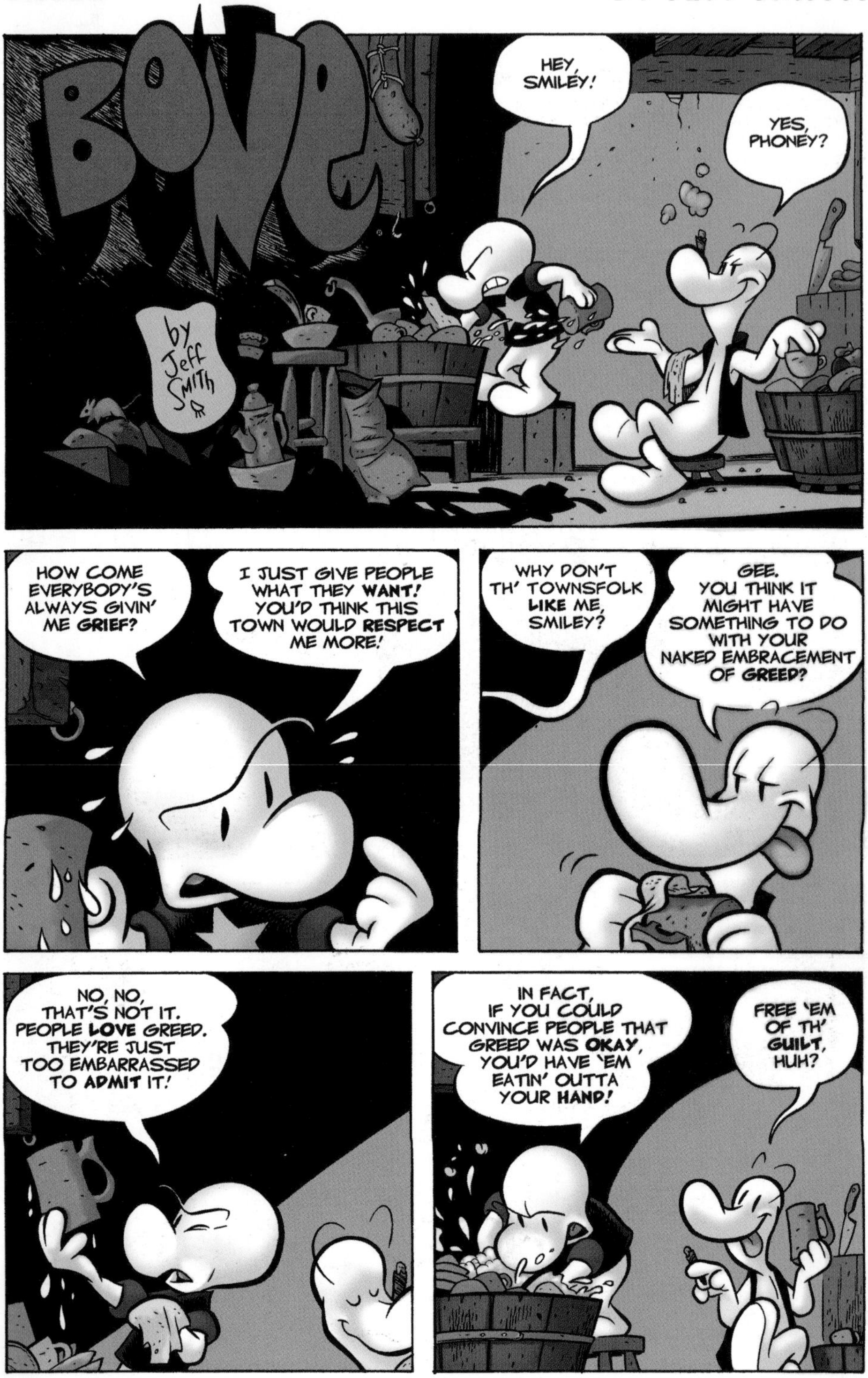
BONE
by Jeff Smith
HEY, SMILEY!
YES, PHONEY?
HOW COME EVERYBODY'S ALWAYS GIVIN' ME GRIEF?
I JUST GIVE PEOPLE WHAT THEY WANT! YOU'D THINK THIS TOWN WOULD RESPECT ME MORE!
WHY DON'T TH' TOWNSFOLK LIKE ME, SMILEY?
GEE. YOU THINK IT MIGHT HAVE SOMETHING TO DO WITH YOUR NAKED EMBRACEMENT OF GREED?
NO, NO, THAT'S NOT IT. PEOPLE LOVE GREED. THEY'RE JUST TOO EMBARRASSED TO ADMIT IT!
IN FACT, IF YOU COULD CONVINCE PEOPLE THAT GREED WAS OKAY, YOU'D HAVE 'EM EATIN' OUTTA YOUR HAND!
FREE 'EM OF TH' GUILT, HUH?

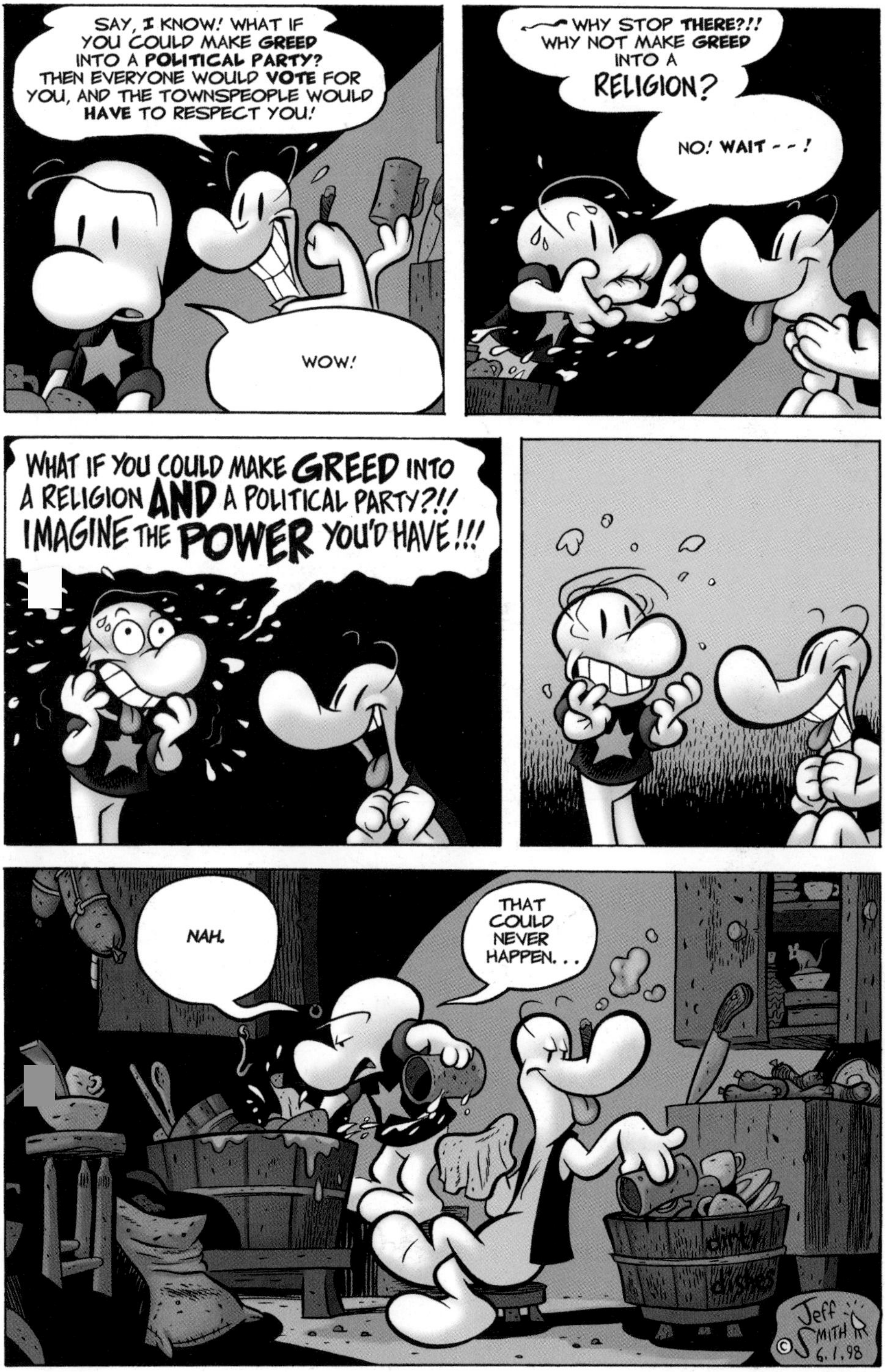
SAY, I KNOW! WHAT IF YOU COULD MAKE GREED INTO A POLITICAL PARTY? THEN EVERYONE WOULD VOTE FOR YOU, AND THE TOWNSPEOPLE WOULD HAVE TO RESPECT YOU!
WOW!
WHY STOP THERE?!! WHY NOT MAKE GREED INTO A RELIGION?
NO! WAIT - - !
WHAT IF YOU COULD MAKE GREED INTO A RELIGION AND A POLITICAL PARTY?!! IMAGINE THE POWER YOU'D HAVE!!!
NAH.
THAT COULD NEVER HAPPEN. . .
Jeff Smith © 6.1.98

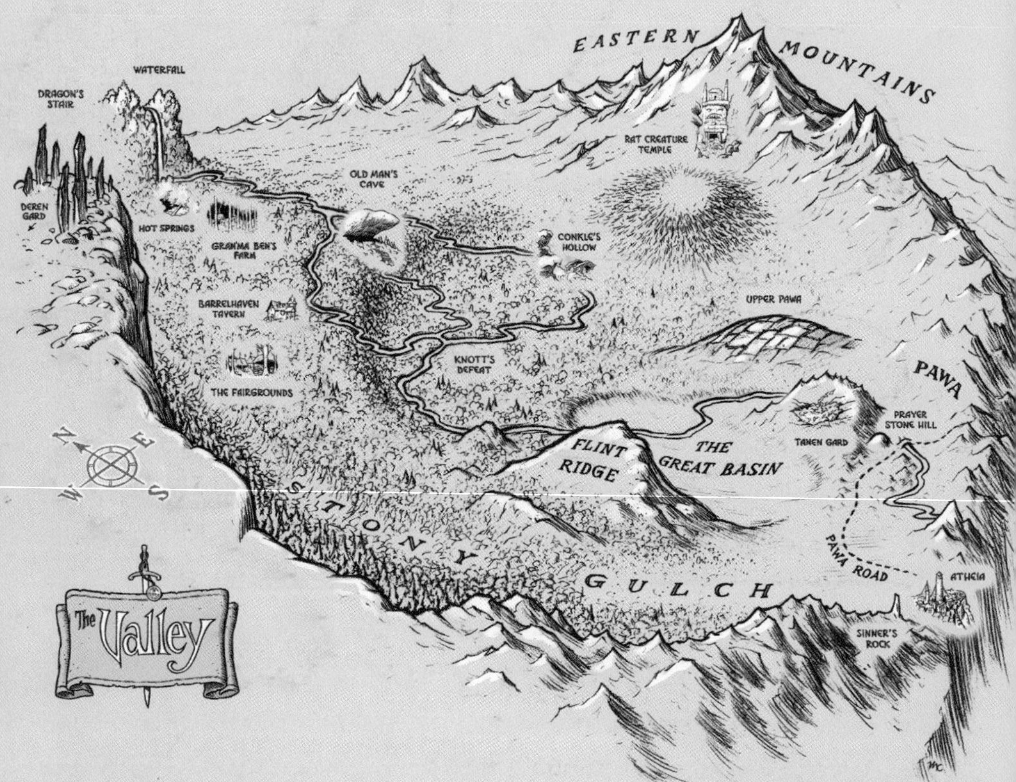
EASTERN MOUNTAINS
WATERFALL
DRAGON'S STAIR
DEREN GARD
HOT SPRINGS
GRAN'MA BEN'S FARM
OLD MAN'S CAVE
CONKLE'S HOLLOW
RAT CREATURE TEMPLE
UPPER PAWA
BARRELHAVEN TAVERN
THE FAIRGROUNDS
KNOTT'S DEFEAT
PAWA
PRAYER STONE HILL
TANEN GARD
FLINT RIDGE
THE GREAT BASIN
STONY GULCH
PAWA ROAD
ATHEIA
SINNER'S ROCK
N
E
S
W
The Valley
MC